The
Billionaire's
Christmas

A SINCLAIR NOVELLA

The Sinclairs

The Billionaire's Christmas (A Sinclair Novella)
No Ordinary Billionaire
The Forbidden Billionaire
The Billionaire's Touch
The Billionaire's Voice
The Billionaire Takes All
The Billionaire's Secrets
Only a Millionaire

The Billionaire's Obsession

Mine for Tonight
Mine for Now
Mine Forever
Mine Completely
Heart of the Billionaire – Sam
Billionaire Undone – Travis
The Billionaire's Salvation – Max
The Billionaire's Game – Kade
Billionaire Unmasked – Jason
Billionaire Untamed – Tate
Billionaire Unbound – Chloe
Billionaire Undaunted – Zane

The Changeling Encounters

The Vampire Coalition

The Billionaire's Christmas

A SINCLAIR NOVELLA

J.S. Scott

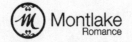 Montlake
Romance

Text copyright © 2014 J. S. SCOTT

Published by Montlake Romance, Seattle

Originally published as "The Billionaire's Angel" in *A Maine Christmas . . . Or Two: A Duet*

www.apub.com

Amazon, the Amazon logo, and Montlake Romance are trademarks of Amazon.com, Inc., or its affiliates.

ISBN 13: 9781542094405
ISBN 10: 1542094402

Cover design by Laura Klynstra

Printed in the United States of America

The
Billionaire's
Christmas

PROLOGUE

Boston, Massachusetts - December 22, 2000

Grady Sinclair pushed a stray lock of hair from his eyes impatiently, straightened his glasses with a frown, and then resumed tapping at lightning speed over the computer keyboard in front of him. He was so close, so very close to solving the problem that he'd been wrestling with on this Internet project. He could feel it, and his intuition always made him doggedly driven to solve the puzzle. In fact, being involved in computer projects was about the only place he felt at home, able to forget that he was imperfect, and so much less than his parents wanted him to be.

"I thought I told you to get your stupid ass downstairs and join the party!" a furious male voice exploded from the doorway of his bedroom, causing Grady to flinch.

Grady froze at the sound of his father's displeasure, although he really should be used to it by now. When it came to his second-born son, Martin Sinclair was always disapproving, and usually downright hostile. "I'm working on something important," he answered his father quietly and carefully, his stomach dropping to his feet because he already knew what his father was going to say.

The large, gray-haired man folded him arms in front of him, his face red with fury. "Every member of this family attends the Sinclair annual Christmas party. Your sister and brothers are doing their duty, while you're up here hiding away like a coward, an embarrassment to the whole Sinclair name, as usual. My son, the idiot, is not at our party because he's too dim-witted to have a conversation. That's what people are saying." Martin stopped to take a wheezing breath before adding, "You'll show yourself downstairs now and try to act like a Sinclair."

Grady tried not to flinch again as he met his father's cold, gray-eyed stare, eyes so very much like his own. "I don't like parties," he stated flatly, knowing it went much deeper than that, but he wasn't about to try to explain. His father had never understood him, and he never would.

"I don't give a shit about what you like and don't like. No son of mine is going to be an idiot *and* a coward. Man up and do what's expected of you," his father growled. "Downstairs. Five minutes. And try not to act like a fool for a change." Martin Sinclair turned around and left without another word.

Grady let out a huge sigh, glad that his father was hosting the annual Christmas party and probably didn't have more time to rake him over the coals for not being the man he wanted *all* of his sons to be.

Martin Sinclair wanted every one of his children to be just like him, and Grady knew he was . . . different. He didn't want to be, but he was, and at the age of eighteen, he knew he'd never be like his father.

Walking to his closet, Grady pulled out a suit and tie, shucking his jeans and T-shirt to put on the more formal clothing. Nothing less than a suit and tie would do, and if he couldn't act like a Sinclair, at least he would dress like one.

The Sinclair annual Christmas party was something he dreaded every year. And by the age of eighteen, he'd attended a lot of them, every one of them torture. He knew his sister and brothers would rally around him for support. His father would say cutting, degrading things, especially as the evening wore on and Martin Sinclair drank more and more alcohol. His father was a mean drunk, even nastier than when he was sober, which wasn't very often. His mother would be the perfect hostess, just like she always was, never naysaying his father. She never did. She was probably as terrified of his father as her children were, but if she was, she never let on. Her plastic smile would stay affixed to her mouth like it was painted on, a smile that would never quite reach her eyes. Sometimes Grady wondered if his mother was really happy. It was hard to tell.

The Sinclairs were old money, and as high in social status as a family could get. His older brother, Evan, was already off to Harvard, home only for Christmas break. Grady envied him, and was counting the days until he could leave for college. Honestly, if he were Evan, he wasn't sure he would come home for breaks at all. Maybe he could make up reasons why he had to stay on campus when he went to college, avoid the humiliation that always occurred at the Christmas parties. The thing was, Evan didn't feel the same revulsion that Grady did over parties and gatherings. In fact, Grady was pretty sure that Evan was probably downstairs charming every person at the party. His brother might not be enjoying himself, but Evan could put on the Sinclair demeanor at will, a trait that Grady admired but couldn't seem to master. All of his siblings could act the part of a proper Sinclair, a talent that Grady would give his right testicle to have. Hell, maybe he'd give up both of them if he could get relief from his father's constant criticism. Grimacing, Grady cupped his genitals, thinking about losing both of his balls. Okay, maybe not *that*. He *was* an eighteen-year-old guy, and that part of his anatomy seemed pretty critical right now. But he'd give *almost* anything to not be the atypical Sinclair in his family. If he could just fit in, he wouldn't draw anyone's notice.

I'm the odd one out, the disappointing Sinclair.

Grady looked in the full-length mirror, straightening his tie and trying to finger-comb his unruly raven hair into place. He was tall, gangly, and awkward, not yet accustomed to how fast his body had grown in the last two years. He thought about taking off his glasses because then he might not look like such a nerd, and maybe if he couldn't see, it might help block out some of the condescending looks from his father and the guests. But then he'd be stumbling around, unable to see things clearly, which would probably make him look that much more clumsy and stupid. He shook his head, knowing his fear was showing in his eyes, and he hated himself for it. If he could see his own terror in the mirror, he knew everyone else would notice it.

I can do this. I can do this. I do it every year.

Grady stiffened his spine and walked through his bedroom door, the noise of the party assaulting him as he descended the stairs.

His palms grew moist and he swallowed hard, trying to dislodge the lump in his throat as he advanced closer to the crowd, a horde of people who he barely knew. And, as usual, they would be unforgiving, laughing at his bizarre behavior, pitying his father for having a pathetic son. His father only mingled with people who had status and wealth, and for the most part, they were as artificial as his father was, and many were just as cruel.

Why do I have to be different? Why can't I just fit in?

Grady could feel his heart thundering against his chest wall, and he tried to control his rapid breathing, willing himself to take slow, deep breaths.

"Don't let them intimidate you, Grady. You're smarter than every one of them." Evan moved up beside him, shoving a plate of food into one of Grady's sweaty hands and a glass of punch into the other. "Just stay busy eating and ignore them."

Hoping the punch was heavily spiked, Grady took a large gulp, his eyes meeting Evan's, nodding with a confidence he wasn't really feeling at the moment.

This is why Evan comes home, even when he doesn't really want to. He comes because of me.

His brother didn't really want to be here either. Grady could sense it. Evan might try to play the badass young businessman to appease their father, but Evan would never come close to being the man their father was, and he didn't enjoy this crowd. Evan was here for one reason and one reason only: to lend support to his younger brother Grady.

One by one, Grady's four siblings surrounded him, none of them speaking, but silently lending support.

Grady remained at the fringe of the crowd, his heart pounding, his dizziness never quite subsiding. He promised himself, at that very moment, that this would be the last Christmas he'd ever suffer through this gathering of vultures who had swooped down and humiliated him every single Christmas since he could remember. He would never, ever go through this again!

As it turned out, Grady kept that vow.

A few hours later, while Grady's father was lecturing his children about everything they'd done wrong during the Christmas party, his eyes rolled back in his head. He clutched his chest, struggling for breath as he fell to the floor, his face diaphoretic and ashen as he took his last breath. Every Sinclair sibling knew that their father was dead, but not a single tear was shed by any of them. Martin Sinclair left each one of his children and his wife exceptionally wealthy, and it *was* the very last Sinclair annual Christmas party.

It was also the year that Grady Sinclair admitted he hated Christmas and always would.

CHAPTER 1

"I can't believe you're really going to approach the Amesport Beast for a donation. You're either very brave or very desperate. Grady Sinclair is the last person who would help you out."

Emily Ashworth glanced up from her seat at her office desk, frowning at her best friend and Youth Center volunteer Randi Tyler. Miranda, better known by everyone in Amesport as Randi, was a local teacher, and volunteered her time at the Center to help kids who needed extra assistance with learning.

"Do I have a choice? He's a billionaire, he lives in Amesport, and we need the money. It's only three weeks until Christmas, and Paul took everything." Emily's eyes drifted down to her computer screen, the balance in the account of the Youth Center of Amesport glaringly showing the numbers in the red. Her ex-boyfriend—if she could even call him *that*—was gone, and so was any money the YCOA had had in the business account. *Damn it!* She should have known Paul was a con, his attention too focused, his pursuit of her too unusual. All his attention and supposed affection was nothing more than a ruse to get his hands on readily available money, funds he shouldn't have been able to steal.

It's my fault. I'm the director. I should have watched him closer, not ever left him alone in my office.

Paul had completely duped her, and she'd stupidly fallen for his con job. The bastard! He'd been in to visit her here at the Center two days ago. She'd had an emergency with one of the kids playing basketball and left him alone for a while in her office. The next day he was gone, and the business account was empty. She'd allowed Paul complete access to the account by rushing away from her desk while the bank account was open on her computer, the password already entered so she could review the accounts.

"It's not your fault," Randi told her soothingly, plopping her jeans-clad butt into the chair in front of the desk. "You had no way of predicting this would happen."

"He always said all the right things, but his compliments were a little contrived, and he seemed nervous and uptight the last time I saw him. I don't know, he just seemed distracted and edgy, but I blew it off as him having a bad day. I should have noticed something wasn't quite right." Emily eyed her petite, dark-haired friend warily, wondering if Randi would have been stupid enough to fall for Paul's smooth lines. Probably not! "No matter whose fault it is, I have to fix this. The Center could go under. And we definitely won't have any funds to buy Christmas presents and food this year for the annual party. The gift from us is the only thing some of these kids get every Christmas." Emily's heart sank to her feet, guilt squeezing at her chest. "I can't let the kids down. I can't let the community down."

Amesport was a small coastal town, but the population of kids who needed this youth center was fairly substantial because of all of the surrounding villages. Losing the Center would be a tough blow to the whole town and the surrounding communities.

Randi rolled her eyes. "So you're just going to walk up to Grady Sinclair's door and ask for money?"

"That's the plan, yes. We can get small donations from the community, but we're missing the whole operating budget for the rest of the year. There's no way to fix this other than to receive a huge donation," Emily replied, sighing as she laid her head down on the desk with her arms underneath it for support, tears of anger and frustration finally escaping from her eyes. "And I don't have the funds to replace it myself."

"I wish I had it to give to you, but I don't have that kind of money lying around either," Randi replied wistfully. "He won't give you the money, so I think you should save yourself the humiliation of asking. Grady Sinclair isn't exactly known for his kindness and generosity. Maybe one of the other Sinclairs—"

"He's the only one in residence. The others are all out of town," Emily replied glumly, aware that the rest of the family, who all had homes on the Amesport Peninsula, were unavailable. She'd already checked. The last thing she really wanted to do was to approach a man who was known for being rude, antisocial, and condescending. But he was the only Sinclair available. So, beast or not, she was asking. Honestly, she probably deserved to have the guy slam the door in her face. This was entirely her fault, even though the police had already told her that this exact same scenario had occurred in several businesses in Maine in the last several months, but they hadn't yet been able to nail the perpetrator. Still, had she not been so completely charmed by Paul's flattering attention, the future of the YCOA wouldn't be in jeopardy.

Men who look like him don't exactly fall all over me. I should have been suspicious! Paul used his looks and charm to bowl me over, and it worked because I'm not used to that kind of male attention.

She was tall, her figure too round, and her long blonde hair was usually scraped back into a ponytail. The old pair of glasses perched on her nose didn't help improve on her blandness, and she wore very little makeup because most of it irritated her skin. She had a tendency to just blend into the woodwork, and men usually made her a buddy rather than a girlfriend.

"Don't cry over Paul. So what if he was attractive? He's a thief and he's definitely not worth it. I'd castrate the bastard if I could find him," Randi said vehemently. "You obviously weren't his first victim, but I'd certainly like to make sure you were his last."

Lifting her head, Emily swiped at the tears on her face. "I'm not upset about *him*. We only dated for a few weeks, and I obviously didn't even know him. But the kids—"

"The kids will survive, and we'll think of something."

The Youth Center was the heart of the town of Amesport. Not only was the sprawling old brick building a refuge for kids of all ages who needed some support and attention, but it was the place where everything important happened, from wedding receptions to weekly events for the senior citizens in the community. Everything good that took place in town happened here, and Emily would be damned if she'd let the community down by letting the Center go under. The people in this town, from the very young to the elderly, needed this gathering place and the activities and services it offered. She hadn't returned to Amesport only to end up destroying the very Center that she herself had used when she was younger.

Amesport had always been *home* to Emily. The only time she had been away was to attend college in California. She'd stayed there for a while after graduation, trying to climb the corporate ladder, before finally realizing that she really didn't give a damn whether or not she reached the top.

As the finance manager of a large charitable corporation, Emily had thought she'd feel good about her job, enjoy working in an environment where helping people came first. Unfortunately, helping people hadn't really been the first thing on the management's agenda, and she hadn't felt good about working for the corporation at all. It had ended up being no different from working for a profitable corporation, the dynamics exactly the same. Sadly, the management had been more interested in politics and kissing up to the right people to get their next promotion than helping anyone.

When her mom had told her the previous director of the Center had retired, Emily had come back home to stay. It had been comforting that very little had changed during her absence, except for the fact that the Sinclair siblings had all decided to finally claim the peninsula outside of town, land that had been in their family for generations. Grady had been the first to build his home there, with all of the other members of the family putting up their own houses after his was completed. As far as she knew, Grady Sinclair was the only full-time resident on the peninsula, but all five of them had houses there, homes that usually sat empty.

"I have to do something," Emily whispered to herself desperately, standing and pulling on her bright red jacket.

"I hear he eats women and small children as snacks," Randi warned her ominously, her lips curving into a small smirk.

Emily smoothed the jacket over her generous hips and retorted, "I think I'd make a decent lunch." Unlike her petite friend, Emily was far from small, and she'd probably make an adequate meal, even for a beast.

She had been back in Amesport and running the YCOA for over a year, but hadn't once encountered a single member of the Sinclair family. Apparently, most of the family was either constantly traveling or lived elsewhere, using their houses here in Maine strictly as vacation homes. Grady Sinclair was rarely spotted in town, but his few not-so-friendly interactions with the locals had labeled him as a complete jerk. Residents here in Amesport weren't accustomed to people being less than polite and friendly; almost anyone in town was more than willing to yack and gossip with a new arrival. Apparently, Grady Sinclair wasn't exactly the amiable type, and Emily wondered why he had ever moved here to Amesport. The Sinclairs were from Boston. Sure, they had land here. But then, they owned real estate just about everywhere.

Randi stood, her smirk replaced by a look of concern as she asked, "Are you sure you want to do this?"

"I'm doing it," Emily answered confidently as she scooped up her purse. "How bad can he be?"

Randi shrugged. "I've actually never met him either. But from what I've heard, he's like the devil incarnate."

Emily rolled her eyes. "Thanks. That's comforting."

Randi grabbed Emily's arm as she made her way to the door and hugged her. "Be careful. Do you want me to go with you?"

Emily was touched that Randi was willing to go confront the beast with her, and she gratefully hugged her friend back. As she released her, she replied, "No. But can you watch over the Center for me? Most of the kids are gone for the evening because there's a storm coming in, but there's a bingo game going on in the recreation hall."

Randi nodded and smiled. "I'll wander over there and lock up when everyone is gone. They usually have good snacks."

Emily gave Randi a mock frown, wishing she had her friend's metabolism and fondness for physical activities. Randi could eat like a horse and never gain an ounce. "Watch yourself. Those ladies get dangerous if you try to swipe too many of their chicken wings," Emily replied with a laugh.

Amused, Randi quipped, "They'll never see me coming or going. I'm an expert at stealing food."

Emily knew Randi meant the comment as a joke, but she knew her friend's background, and didn't doubt there was some real truth in Randi's statement.

"Thanks," Emily told her friend quietly.

Randi gave her a mock salute and a grin as she walked off toward the recreation room.

Emily sighed heavily as she made her way to the exit door, trying not to cringe at the thought of approaching Grady Sinclair. She'd gone up against some intimidating men during her time in California. Sure, he was a billionaire, but he was just a man, right? No different from any other rich guy she'd encountered in her corporate job.

It was dark and snowing as she drove her ancient truck toward the peninsula, knowing it was way past time for new tires, but they weren't really in her budget. Honestly, she bought very little unless it was a necessity. With the cost of paying back student loans, and the low salary she was receiving for her current job, almost everything was beyond her means. She could make more money with her business degree somewhere else, but she'd rather do without than go back into corporate business. She just didn't have the killer instinct to move up the corporate ladder while she was taking someone else down to get there. All she really wanted was to be in a job where she could do something good. And she'd found that at the Center. Unfortunately, she'd made the mistake of dating the wrong guy, which was the story of her life. Granted, the money he'd made off with hadn't been a fortune, but it was a lot to her, money she just didn't have to replace. It was the funds for the expenses of the Center for December, and all the money that had been raised throughout the year for the Christmas festivities. And the sum was way more than she could afford, or hope to get in donations.

"Fat chance the police will have any luck," Emily muttered to herself as she pulled up to the gate that blocked the road to the peninsula. Paul had disappeared as though he had never existed. The police had investigated, but had very little information. Paul probably wasn't even his real name, and he had done this several times before without being caught—if the similar incidents were done by the same man.

Swallowing hard, she stared at the massive metal gate in front of her, wondering how she was going to actually get through it, when the decorative doors started to swing open soundlessly.

It's not locked or guarded. It's motion operated.

Okay. *That* surprised her. In fact, it took her a moment to even give the truck some gas to enter through the open gate. When she finally came out of her perplexed trance, she gunned the engine, making the back end of the truck fishtail on her bald tires. She straightened her vehicle up and kept going. The snow was coming down heavier, a sloppy, wet snow with high winds that signaled an incoming nor'easter.

What did I expect? A guarded fortress?

But yeah, actually, she had assumed there would be some sort of barrier between the ultrarich Sinclair family and the rest of the world. Even though the peninsula wasn't that large, the Sinclairs owned the entire cape, and the road was private. To be allowed to enter just by driving up to the gate *was* a surprise. When she was a child, the projecting mass of land had sat empty, and she had ignored the No Trespassing signs more times than she could remember to sit out on one of the shorelines, her very favorite spot on the headland.

My favorite place is in the exact same spot where Grady Sinclair built his house.

Emily couldn't see well, but she squinted into the swirling snow and pushed her glasses back up onto the bridge of her nose. Passing several private driveways, she kept on going, knowing Grady's home was the very last one.

The road ended at his house, and Emily forged ahead, parking her truck in the circular driveway and turning off the engine.

I must be insane!

Before she had time to think about what she was doing and leave, Emily grabbed her purse and slammed the door of the truck closed. Glad she was dressed in a sweater and jeans for the weather, she just wished she were also wearing a pair of boots, her sneakers slipping and sliding in the fresh, wet snow.

The house was massive, and she gaped at the heavy oak doors in front of her, wanting to run away as fast as her slippery shoes would take her.

"What kind of single guy owns a house this humungous?" she whispered in awe.

Answering herself, she said, "A man who has enough money to donate to the Youth Center."

With that thought in mind, she strode determinedly forward and pressed the doorbell harder than she needed to, causing her feet to slide out from under her and her body to land ungracefully in a heap on Grady Sinclair's doorstep.

That was a fabulous and graceful entrance, Emily. Impress him with your professionalism.

Disgusted with herself, she scrambled for purchase on the icy stone porch, hastily trying to get to her feet before he answered the door, but she slid again and landed flat on her rear end, flinching as her tailbone hit the unyielding surface. "Damn!"

Abruptly, the door swung open, and Emily Ashworth got her first look at the beast from an undignified position on her frozen ass.

Her glasses were wet and foggy, but he looked like no beast she had ever seen. He did, however, look pretty fierce, dark, and dangerous. Without saying a word, Grady Sinclair stuck his hand out as though he completely expected her to take it. She did, grasping his hand as he pulled her to her feet like she was as light as a feather. Trying to straighten up quickly to regain some modicum of dignity, she gawked up at him. She was tall for a woman, but he dwarfed her, towering over her menacingly. He was dressed informally in a tan thermal shirt that stretched across rippling muscles and a massive chest. He was sporting a pair of jeans that looked worn, and he filled them out in a way she'd never seen a man wear a pair of jeans before.

Holy crap! Grady Sinclair was hot. Scorching hot. His dark hair was mussed, and he had a just-rolled-out-of-bed look that made her want to drag him back to a bedroom. Any bedroom. He looked like he hadn't shaved today, and the dark, masculine stubble on his jaw just added to the testosterone waves she swore she could almost feel pulsating from his magnificent body and entering hers, making her squirm just a little at her body's reaction to him.

She drew in a deep breath as his gray-eyed stare seemed to assess her, and finally came to rest on her face. "Hi," she said weakly, unable to form any intelligent words right at that moment. Her brain was mush and her cheeks flushed pink with mortification. This just wasn't the businesslike, graceful entrance she had hoped for, and her lustful reaction to Grady Sinclair had her uncharacteristically flustered.

I need to get it together. I'm acting like an idiot. I need this donation.

He grabbed a fistful of her jacket and tugged her inside, closing the door behind her. Plucking the glasses from her face, he used his shirt to clean them before he handed them back to her. "You don't look like one of my brother Jared's usual women," he said gruffly. "Bedroom is upstairs." He pointed his thumb toward the spiral staircase on the far side of the enormous front room.

Emily stared at him blankly for a moment, and then slanted her gaze toward the living room to try to clear her head. She certainly couldn't seem to think straight when she was looking directly at *him*.

Bedroom? What the hell is he talking about? Jared's women?

"I think you have me mistaken for someone else. I don't know you, and I'm not acquainted with Jared. I came to ask a favor." *Who does he think I am?*

"And you're offering *your* favors for a favor, right?" he asked grimly, his graveled baritone almost disapproving.

Her head jerked back to his face. "What? No. What kind of favor?" she replied suspiciously.

"My brother Jared told me I needed to get laid, which generally is followed by a woman arriving here at my house. I usually just send the women away with a check. But I've decided I'll take you," he said huskily.

Emily gulped. "Someone sends you women . . . as in prostitutes?" Good God, the last thing Grady Sinclair needed was a hooker. She couldn't think of one single woman who would actually turn him down. "Do I look like a whore?" she asked irritably, suddenly offended by the fact that he'd thought she was for sale. But she felt a shiver of need slide down her spine and land right between her thighs at the thought that he actually wanted her, and what he might do to her if she *were* actually a woman for hire. She wasn't beautiful and she was curvy, her ample figure a little more than most men found attractive.

He reached out and unzipped her jacket, divesting her of the garment and hanging it on a hook by the door. Turning back to her, he said slowly, "Nope. You don't. That's why I want to fuck you."

Emily gasped, his blatant words and heated appraisal making her flush. "Well, I don't know Jared, and I don't want to do *that*." *Liar. Liar.* She so *did* want to do *that*, but she wasn't about to admit it when he'd just insulted her. Besides, she didn't do casual sex. "I'm Emily Ashworth and I'm the director of the Youth Center of Amesport. I wanted to talk to you about a possible donation."

She shuddered as his intense, molten gaze swept over her body and back to her face, staring at her with a look so smoldering and hungry that her core clenched in response.

"You're cold," he said abruptly, taking her frozen hand in his and leading her through the living room, down the hallway and into a cheery kitchen. "Sit," he demanded huskily as he dropped her hand, halting at the kitchen table.

Emily sat, so confused that she was unable to make herself do anything else. She watched silently as Grady Sinclair moved around the kitchen, his large body maneuvering with a fluidity of motion that shouldn't be possible for a man as large and muscular as he was. Watching him from behind was almost mesmerizing. She was jealous of the denim that was cupping an ass so tight that she could see the flex of muscle beneath the seat of his jeans as he moved, and it was a view she couldn't bring herself to look away from for some time. Finally, ripping her gaze from him, she let her eyes wander around the kitchen—a bright, airy room with beautiful granite countertops and polished wood floors. The all-white kitchen had high-end appliances that Emily eyed covetously and gleaming copper pots hanging from hooks on the ceiling. Beyond, there was a dining room with a formal, polished wood table, but the room was dim, sparsely furnished, and looked seldom used.

He sauntered to the kitchen table moments later and pushed a mug in front of her, sitting down next to her with his own cup in hand. Emily placed her cold fingers around the mug, sighing as she inhaled the heated, fragrant brew. It was a hot apple cider, and she took a long sip, the warm liquid instantly starting to thaw out her frigid body. "Thank you," she told him quietly as she set her mug back on the table. "So will you consider it?"

"Why?" he questioned darkly, his heated gaze spearing her as she squirmed uncomfortably in her chair.

"The Center needs money."

"Why?" he asked again, lifting a brow as he sipped his drink, his eyes never leaving her.

He knows I'm desperate, that there's a reason I'm here so late asking for money.

"A man I was dating stole the operating money from the Center and we can't keep running without a significant donation," she admitted, wondering why she was feeling the need to be completely honest with him.

Starting hesitantly, she spilled the entire story about the money being stolen as Grady watched her, his expression unreadable as he listened. "So would you be willing to help?" she asked nervously as she finished her story.

He was silent, his expression contemplative as he continued to look at her. Intense minutes passed before he finally answered, "I might be willing to consider it. But I'd want something in return."

She picked up her mug and took another sip of cider, swallowing awkwardly before she spoke again. "What? I'll do whatever I can to get you what you want." The whole future of Amesport depended on his answer. Emily knew she had nowhere else to go and no other solution.

"That's good, because you're the only one who can get it for me," he agreed casually. "Because what I really want is *you*."

Emily nearly choked, sputtering as she swallowed. Dear God, maybe Grady Sinclair *was* the Amesport Beast after all. "I need to give the town of Amesport a Christmas, they need the Center to stay open, and I'll do anything to keep from disappointing the kids there, but I'm not sleeping with you to do it," she told him indignantly.

"We don't need to sleep," Grady replied gruffly. "And I hate Christmas."

How could he hate Christmas? Who hated Christmas except Scrooge?

Emily looked around the massive, tastefully decorated home: not a single red or green decoration in sight. She hadn't seen one Christmas item in his living room, and there was nothing in the dining room or kitchen. "I happen to love Christmas. It's the season of giving and helping others, a time of forgiveness and good cheer."

"Not in my experience," Grady replied, rising from his chair to take his mug to the sink. "It's a time of commercial greed where everyone expects something. Nobody is really happy. It's not real. People are doing what they think is expected of them."

Emily stood up and stalked over to him, rinsed out both mugs in the sink, and placed them in the dishwasher. "It's the happiest time of the year." Emily placed her hands on her hips and stared up at Grady, wondering what had made him so cynical. Her irritation drained away as she caught a glimpse of vulnerability in his eyes, a look that told her he wasn't being cruel. He was telling her what Christmas had been like for *him*, and for just a moment, Emily had the craziest compulsion to wrap her arms around him and show him that not everyone in the world wanted something from him.

But even I want something from him. I want funds for the Center.

"I can't have sex with you for money, Mr. Sinclair," Emily told him flatly.

"I'll donate a million dollars," he said huskily, his large body moving closer, pinning her between his body and the sink. "And I'm Grady. I don't want you calling me Mr. Sinclair. Too many of us."

"I can't," she whispered quietly, almost regretting her ethics. "And nobody donates a million dollars to the YCOA."

"I would," he rumbled.

His scent surrounded her as his hands landed on the edge of the sink, a fragrance so masculine that it was intoxicating her. Grady smelled like the ocean, pine, and a tantalizing musk that was uniquely *him*.

Their gazes locked and held; time suspended as Emily began drowning in the swirling, molten pools of gray that reminded her of a storm coming off the ocean. He captured her in the same way as a violent storm, her heart racing as she waited for a force of nature that seemed inevitable.

She didn't really believe he'd donate a million bucks to her Center just to sleep with her, but she'd never seen a man look at her like this, like he needed to have her or die. Unfortunately, Emily had a feeling that she was gazing at him exactly the same way.

"The boyfriend who stole from you . . . did you love him?" Grady growled, his face a mask of ambivalence, but his eyes were saying something completely different.

"We were only dating for a few weeks. And no, I didn't love him. Obviously he was only after money. He wasn't interested in me." It hurt, but Emily knew it was true. She had been a pawn in Paul's game, a nonperson who was disposable.

"Did you fuck him?" Grady asked bluntly.

"No. Of course not. I barely knew him," Emily replied, offended.

"Good." A satisfied look replaced his severe expression. "He was an asshole."

Grady had moved so close that she could feel his warm breath on her cheek, his close proximity making her quiver with need.

"Please," she whispered, although she didn't have a clue what she really wanted. All she knew was that she was caught up in some crazy compulsion that she couldn't seem to break away from. She wrapped her arms around his neck, still held in thrall by the scent of him, the feel of his muscular body pressed against hers.

Without another word, Grady lowered his head and took her mouth with his, and she suddenly knew exactly what she had wanted. Emily surrendered to him with a wanton moan, losing herself completely to the beast.

CHAPTER 2

Grady had known he wanted the woman in his arms from the moment he'd seen her sitting on her ass on his doorstep, looking up at him with those innocent blue eyes through crooked glasses, and an embarrassed expression. Emily Ashworth had looked like an angel that had crash-landed on his porch, and he'd been disappointed when he remembered that Jared had threatened to send him another hookup. That had been the last thing he'd wanted . . . until he saw Emily. His cock had jumped to attention almost immediately, and all he'd wanted to do was seize the woman, throw her over his shoulder, and make her his as quickly as humanly possible.

Mine.

Spearing his hands through her hair, he groaned into her mouth as the tie holding her hair back gave way, spilling the silky strands over his fingers, caressing his hands like a lover. He felt greedy and desperate, his mouth tasting, his tongue trying to claim her. She tasted like ambrosia, and he couldn't get enough. All he wanted to do was devour her whole, but she'd already said no, which made him even more frenzied. There was something about this woman that was seeping into his skin as he held her, melting the ice around his heart, and starting to relieve the restlessness and loneliness that were his constant companions. It was as exhilarating as it was frightening.

I'm happy being alone. I do what I want, when I want. I like it that way.

Grady was lying to himself, and he knew it. Panicked, he lifted his mouth from hers, an effort that was nearly superhuman.

Fuck. Fuck. Fuck. Separating himself from her that abruptly had been painful.

Glancing down at her just-been-thoroughly-ravaged look, Grady fought not to swoop down on her again and lose himself in her heat all over again.

What the fuck is wrong with me?

"Give me a week, and I'll give you a million dollars." The impulsive comment sprang from his mouth without him thinking about it. "No sex, but I want you to stay here at the house. Just show me Christmas." He was no longer interested in a quick screw for money. Not from her, not from Emily. But he was desperate to get her close to him and keep her there.

Grady's heart was thundering, and his breath was coming heavy in and out of his lungs.

Say yes!

He watched as her brows crinkled in a thoughtful expression. "How?" she whispered in a low, *fuck-me* voice that nearly made him come undone.

He shrugged. "I don't know. I haven't really ever celebrated Christmas. Not the way normal people do, anyway. Make me see it the way you do. Do whatever you usually do here with me."

Oh, hell yeah. He wanted this woman near him, for as long as he could keep her here. His enormous house felt different with her here. *He* felt different.

"You'll really donate money to the Center if I spend a week with you?" she asked, as though she were confused by the whole idea.

"You're not involved with someone else, right?" The question came out casually, but Grady's heart clenched at the thought. Granted, the guy she was dating had just hauled ass with all her money, but there *could* be someone else.

"No. There was just the thief, and even he didn't really want me," she replied sadly, her eyes breaking contact with his to land in the center of his chest.

Grady wanted to break every bone in the asshole's body. His arms came up to stroke her back and he pulled her against him as though he could protect her from the world. How any man could push this woman away was beyond him. "Was he caught?"

"No," she replied despairingly.

"Give me his information. I'll find him."

"The police can't track him. They're sure it was a false identity."

"I will," Grady vowed confidently. He had so many connections that there was nobody he couldn't track down. "In the meantime, I'll give you the money and you give me your word that you'll spend Christmas with me. What about your family?"

"Only child, a late-in-life surprise for my parents," she replied in a muffled voice against his chest. "Mom and Dad are snowbirds now. They spend the winter in Florida. I couldn't go this year."

The sorrow in her voice made Grady determined to make this the best Christmas season she'd ever had. So what if he personally hated the holidays? Emily obviously didn't, and she was alone this year, just like him. "Then spend it here with me."

She pulled her head back and looked at him with an earnest expression as she asked, "Why me? Why this?"

"Because it's what I want," he answered, knowing it was the truth. "And you said you'd give me what I wanted."

"You promise no sex?" she asked hesitantly.

"Only if you beg," he answered arrogantly, although he was starting to wonder if he might end up being the one pleading. Her sweetness tempted him, and he was going to have a very hard time trying not to devour her.

Pulling away from him, he saw her roll her eyes at his bravado, and it brought an involuntary smile to his lips.

"You have a deal. But I'm bringing a tree and all of my Christmas decorations here," she told him in a threatening voice as he followed her toward the door. "And the Center has a big Christmas party that I'll need and want to attend. You can come with me if you like. If you're donating, it will mean a lot. We can save the annual party. It's important, especially for the kids."

Great. He could hardly wait. He avoided red-and-green decorations like the plague. But if it would bring her back, she could plaster them in every corner of his house, as long as *she* came along with the red bows and mistletoe.

He helped her into her coat and slammed his feet into his heavy boots, grabbing a jacket from the closet and putting it on as he followed her out of the house.

"This is what you're driving?" he said irritably, his eyes roaming over the bald tires on the small truck. "It looks like a goddamn death trap."

The ground was covered in a couple inches of snow, wet and slippery moisture that would have her sliding everywhere on the roads.

"I know how to drive in snow," she replied stubbornly as she opened the door of her truck.

"You need a new vehicle," he replied in a surly tone. She couldn't be driving on the road in this piece of shit. Slapping a hand on the window of her truck, he slammed the door closed and dug in his pocket, bringing out a set of keys. "Drive my truck. It's too slick to drive around with those tires. There's no tread left."

"I can still get some mileage out of them," Emily retorted snappishly. "They aren't that bad."

She was defensive, and Grady immediately knew that she probably couldn't afford it. "Don't you get paid?"

"Not much," she admitted with a sigh. "But I like my job."

"Drive my truck or our deal is off," he grumbled, dangling the set of keys in front of her face.

"I can't take your vehicle," she protested adamantly.

He shrugged. "I have several." He pointed to a huge truck on the other side of the circular drive. "Get into the truck, Emily."

She took the keys reluctantly, drawing a breath to argue as her feet started to skid. Grady scooped her up and bodily carried her to his truck. "Open the door," he ordered, not giving her a chance to argue. She pulled the heavy door open and he deposited her in the driver's seat. "Be careful," he demanded after giving her a rundown of where everything was in the vehicle. "There isn't a lot of snow, but it's slippery. Call me when you get home safe."

"I don't have your number," she said, shaking her head.

"Cell phone," he ordered, holding out his hand.

Emily dug in her purse and handed it to him.

He programmed his number in, called his own number with her phone just long enough to register her phone number, and then handed it back to her. "Now you have my number." Digging in the pocket of his jeans, he pulled out a business card from his wallet and handed it to her. "Take this too." He wanted her to have anything with his name on it, anything to remind her of him, and his contact information available everywhere.

"Are you really sure—"

"I'll have the money transferred into the YCOA account tomorrow. Get me the bank account number." He wasn't about to give her time to second-guess her decision. Hell, he'd wire the money right now if he thought it would get her locked into the deal tighter. "You look tired. You need sleep." He could see the worry showing on her face, and tiny black circles under her eyes. He didn't like it. The desire to see her happy was almost a compulsion, and he was damn near ready to do almost anything to see her smile and remove the signs of stress on her beautiful face.

She shook her head, exasperated, and tucked the card into her purse. "Does anyone ever argue with you or refuse you?" she asked curiously.

"I don't usually ask for anything," he answered bluntly, unable to stop himself from swooping down and kissing her. Her lips warmed beneath his, and Grady wanted to drag her back into the house and warm every part of her body until she begged for mercy. But he stepped back and looked away, closing the door of the truck so she wouldn't get too cold, his protective instincts stronger than his own desire.

He watched the taillights disappear down the road, knowing his life had just changed completely, and he wasn't sure what, if anything, he was going to do about it.

Grady trudged slowly back into the house, divesting himself of his boots and jacket in the foyer, and made his way into his home office.

Picking up the phone, he hoped that Simon Hudson was at home. The two of them had met several years ago, and had become friends almost immediately. Simon had very successfully launched a line of computer games that were still a sensation, while Simon's business partner and brother, Sam, had started a branch of the company that specialized in investments and venture capitalism, the same thing that Evan had done to turn his multimillionaire status into a billionaire title. Grady and Simon had connected because they were so much alike back then, both of them reclusive computer nerds. But since Simon had met and married his wife, Kara, who had recently delivered a baby, Simon wasn't the same guy anymore. At one time, Simon's only love had been his computer and his focused drive to design the most challenging computer games on the market. And he'd more than achieved that goal. But now, Simon was completely and totally obsessed with his wife and child. Grady had hoped Simon would get over it, the newness of his relationship wearing off after a while, and turn back into the sensible friend he had known before Simon had met Kara. It didn't happen, and although he and Simon still talked, Grady couldn't begin to understand his friend's obsession with a woman. Until now.

Picking up the phone in his office, Grady hit the speed dial, thinking that if anyone could understand an almost immediate obsession with a female, it was Simon Hudson.

Grady ignored Simon's abrupt greeting and blurted out immediately, "There's something seriously wrong with me. I met this woman today and now I don't feel like myself anymore. I felt literally nauseous when she left. Shit! Maybe I'm getting the flu. What the hell do I do now?" Grady finished with a huff, his air completely gone.

Simon was silent for a moment before Grady finally heard an evil laugh on the other end of the line. Grady plopped into his office chair and propped his feet on the desk, waiting for Simon to stop laughing uproariously.

"Marry her," Simon replied, his voice actually jovial. "Don't turn yourself inside out like I did. Throw her over your shoulder and take her, kicking and screaming if you need to, and find the nearest justice of the peace. Put yourself out of your misery early, buddy."

"I just met the woman," Grady answered irritably.

"Doesn't matter. If she's already making you crazy, you're screwed. Would you be willing to do anything just to see her again?" Simon questioned mildly.

"A million bucks," Grady admitted. "I offered to donate a million dollars to her charity to spend Christmas with her."

Simon whistled. "You got it bad. You hate Christmas."

"I know," Grady answered wretchedly. "But she wouldn't fuck me, so I was desperate."

"Trust me, the fucking just makes it even worse. Then you'll want her all the time, every minute of the day." Simon hesitated before asking, "Is she worth it?"

Grady thought about that for a minute, remembering Emily's vulnerable expression and how happy he had felt just looking at her and feeling her body pressed against him. "I think so. I mean, I just met her, so I guess it's hard to tell. She seems to take away the loneliness and she made me smile. She's"—he paused for a moment before finishing— "different. Not like any woman I've ever met. She wanted a donation for her organization, but she didn't seem interested in anything for herself. She refused to fuck me for money. And I was actually happy about that. Why the hell would I be happy? I wanted her horizontal."

"Maybe because you want her to like you?" Simon mused.

"Nobody likes me except you," Grady answered harshly.

"Who says I like you? You can be a real asshole sometimes," Simon answered, amused.

"And you aren't?" Grady shot back automatically, used to sparring with Simon.

"I say if she can put up with your ornery ass, just marry her. It took me thirty-three years to find a woman who could tolerate me," Simon replied happily.

"I'm only thirty-one. And I think your marriage is a little more than that," Grady said, swinging his feet off the desk and swiveling around uncomfortably in his chair. He'd never talked to Simon about Kara much because he'd never understood his friend's obsession with her.

"Yep. She loves me, and I'm a lucky bastard," Simon answered, his tone cocky.

Grady hesitated for a moment before asking reluctantly, "Does it ever go away? You know, the possessive, crazy feeling you get when you first meet a woman who makes you feel that way."

"No," Simon answered seriously. "It doesn't. It gets worse the closer you get to her. But it's worth it if she cares about you in the same way. You'll never feel lonely again, buddy."

Grady contemplated Simon's words for a while, wondering exactly what *that* would feel like. He was close to his sister and brothers, but they all had their own lives, and were rarely together. What would it be like to truly feel like he wasn't alone, to really feel like he was connected to someone who made him feel complete? He'd actually never thought about it before, had never been exactly unhappy with his life, but he'd always known that there was *something* missing. There was a gaping hole somewhere inside him that not even his computers or his siblings could fill, and meeting Emily had somehow made that emptiness seem suddenly pretty damn painful.

"Tell me what it was like with Kara," Grady asked Simon quietly, wanting to hear about what Simon had gone through before he'd finally found happiness. He and Simon were friends, but they usually discussed computers. Grady had reached billionaire status by developing several wildly successful businesses online and then selling them off, and their conversation almost always revolved around work.

Maybe that's because that's all I do.

But his mind wasn't on work, and he wanted to talk about Simon's life, and the wife who had changed his friend so profoundly.

Surprisingly, Simon began to talk, and he didn't stop for over an hour, barely taking a breath, launching into one story after another. Once started, Simon couldn't seem to stop talking about Kara and his new baby girl.

By the time Grady hung up, he wasn't sure if he should be terrified or relieved. Being alone seemed so much easier and so much less complicated than tying himself up in knots over a female like Simon had done.

Then again, I'm not happy like Simon either.

Glancing up at the clock, he realized how much time had passed since Emily had left. Getting up, he looked outside. The nor'easter had definitely arrived in full force. The wind was howling and the snow was whirling around badly enough to be blinding.

She didn't call me.

Visions of Emily hurt or stranded somewhere started racing through his mind, one horrible scenario after the other.

Panicked, he picked up his cell phone and programmed in the number he'd gotten from her earlier. He then put the phone back in his pocket and paced the office like a caged lion, checking outside about every ten seconds.

She'll call. She probably just got busy.

"Fuck it!" Grady whispered harshly to himself after he'd waited longer than he could handle, pulling the phone from his pocket and punching her number.

He'd managed to wait exactly two minutes from the time he'd hung up with Simon before calling Emily to make sure she was safely home.

"Hello," Emily answered, sounding breathless.

Grady's worry turned to relief. "You didn't call me," he grumbled irritably. "You were supposed to let me know you were home safe."

"I just got home. I had to run errands," Emily told him matter-of-factly. "I'm sorry. Were you worried?"

He should say no. He could tell her that he just got a free minute, so that's why he was calling now. He should be nonchalant, not let her know he was actually having visions of her bloodied and stranded somewhere. There were many excuses he could have given for jumping the gun on the phone call, but he simply answered, "Yeah. A little. It's been a while since you left." For some reason, he didn't want to lie to Emily.

"I'm home now." The sound of a slamming door confirmed her statement. "Thank you for caring that I got home safe. It's very thoughtful."

He should tell her that he wasn't thoughtful at all. He was a self-centered bastard who couldn't stand the thought of her hurting or stranded somewhere because he selfishly wanted her. But he didn't tell her that. He liked that aching sweetness of her comment too much. Simon was right. Grady did want Emily to like him. "What did you get?" he asked curiously, hearing the sound of rustling bags in the background while she was silent.

"Household stuff. Nothing exciting," she answered with a laugh. "Boring stuff that you wouldn't find very interesting."

He found *everything* about her interesting. Grady plopped his ass into a recliner, thinking that every little thing about Emily fascinated him. He wanted to know what she'd bought, where she'd stopped, what kind of things she liked. And he wanted to keep hearing that husky, sexy laugh of hers all damn night. "I'm interested. Tell me." Right at the moment, he just wanted to hear her voice. It might make him harder than a rock, but it also soothed him.

He wasn't disappointed. Emily started talking. He eventually got the account information for the Center, but they just kept talking after that. Grady's restlessness slowly faded away as he got lost in the conversation.

CHAPTER 3

The million-dollar deposit was in the YCOA account the very next morning. In fact, it was deposited shortly after Emily arrived at work. She'd stared at the balance for the Center, stunned, for almost fifteen minutes before she logged out of the bank account. Grady had actually done it. He'd made a million-dollar donation.

The package came in the afternoon, delivered by a teenager who actually worked at the local florist but had agreed to do an extra delivery for one of the town's optometrists, Dr. Pope. The sandy-haired boy had winked at her when he delivered it, telling her cheekily that it was a delivery that had paid very well when she had started digging for money to tip him, which he'd refused.

Turning the package over and over, Emily couldn't figure out *why* she was getting a delivery, but her name was on it, and the delivery boy had been told specifically to deliver it to her personally.

She tore open the large manila envelope and groped inside, pulling out the contents carefully and letting the items fall onto the surface of her desk. There were two cases, and she popped open the first one and froze for a moment, staring at a dainty pair of glasses in an adorably feminine frame. She'd actually tried them on in Dr. Pope's office and rejected the choice, reasoning that they were too impractical, but the real reason she'd decided against them had been the cost. They were much fancier and definitely more expensive than something she would have chosen. *What the hell?* Yanking off her regular glasses, she slid the new pair onto her face, the world around her coming into much better focus. Her glasses were old, and they had surface scratches, but she'd lost one of her contact lenses a few months ago and was waiting until she could afford to get more. Snapping open the other case, she wasn't particularly surprised to see that several pair of contacts were in the case, and she was positive they were exactly the right prescription. Dr. Pope knew exactly what she needed. She'd just had her eye exam a few months ago, and was waiting until she could afford what she required to correct her vision properly.

Emily squealed loud enough to bring Randi running into her office, the brunette's face panicked. "What happened?" she asked breathlessly.

"I got new glasses. And contacts. I can't believe my mom and dad did this for me. They live on a fixed income. They really can't afford it." Emily's eyes started to tear at the thought of her parents sacrificing for her. She didn't even remember telling them she had lost her old contacts. Usually she avoided bad news. Her parents were getting on in years, and she tried to keep to the happier stuff when she spoke with them because they worried.

Randi came to the desk and sifted through the contents. "Um . . . Em . . . I don't think it was from your parents." Randi dangled a card from her fingertips before handing it to Emily.

It was Dr. Pope's card, but on the back, written in script, was Grady Sinclair's name and the word *Paid*.

"Grady? Why?" she whispered to herself, running her index finger over the card.

Randi raised a brow, asking curiously, "Is there something you haven't told me about your little visit with Grady Sinclair?"

Emily had asked Randi earlier not to ever refer to Grady by anything other than his name. He'd saved her ass, asking for very little in return except her company for Christmas. And why he wanted *that* she still hadn't figured out. "No. We talked. He made me drive his truck because he was worried about my bad tires. And I left." Okay, she was omitting the tiny little detail that Grady had mistaken her for a woman who traded sex for money. And she wasn't about to mention the fact that he'd kissed her. Knowing Randi, she'd blow the whole thing out of proportion. It was just . . . a kiss. It wasn't like Grady Sinclair actually had any real interest in *her*.

"Obviously you made quite an impression," Randi answered in a teasing voice.

"I can't keep these. Why did he do this?" Emily pulled off the new glasses.

"You need them. Keep them." Reaching out stealthily, Randi snatched Emily's old glasses away from her and put them in her pocket. "Just so you know, these are going to go missing unless you absolutely need them for some kind of emergency. And now . . . you don't need them." Chuckling softly, Randi scampered out of Emily's office.

"Miranda Tyler, bring those back here." Emily put the new glasses back on and followed Randi, only to find that Randi had grabbed her stuff and left like her ass was on fire.

"Damn." Emily plopped back into her chair in the office. Would they even let her return the glasses now that they had been made for her? Probably not. And she'd be hard-pressed to come up with the money to pay them off.

Grady paid. I have to pay him. Why did he do it?

Emily dug through her purse and pulled out Grady's card. He'd called her last night, sounding almost upset that she hadn't already called him to let him know she'd made it home. Stopping at the grocery store first, she had just been coming through the door when her cell phone rang. He'd gotten the number for the Center's bank account, and then they had talked about everything and nothing for two hours. He was a good listener, and he prompted her to talk about her parents and what it was like growing up in Amesport, and he asked a lot of questions about the programs at the Center. Surprisingly, he'd seemed to genuinely care about the impact of the programs on the community. Grady Sinclair was blunt, gruff, and, okay, maybe he could be a bit abrupt and intimidating, but the problem was . . . she actually liked him. His public image was all wrong, and Grady was a complete fraud. Underneath his rough exterior was a man with a good heart. Emily was almost certain of that. There was no artificial charm or smoothness to Grady, and that made him that much hotter. He was all male, all the time, and everything feminine inside her reacted to that, reacted to him.

Shaking her head at her own foolishness, she laid his card on the desk and brought up her e-mail.

> Dear Mr. Sinclair,
>
> Thank you for your generous donation to the Youth Center of Amesport.
>
> I am in receipt of the package you sent today. I hope you will be able to accept payment arrangements for the contents. Although I was planning to purchase some products I needed from Dr. Pope, I hadn't planned to buy all this right now. It's an unexpected expense that I haven't budgeted to purchase. Can I make monthly payments to you?
>
> Regards,
> Emily Ashworth

His reply came through within a few minutes.

Emily,

Your glasses are scratched and you need them. I used to wear glasses when I was younger, and trying to see around scratches is annoying. If you try to pay me, I'll find a way to get my donation back. And there is no Mr. Sinclair at this e-mail address.

G.

Emily knew she should be angry, but she actually burst out laughing at his reply. There was no professional politeness with Grady. He got right to the point. She sent a lightning-fast reply.

Mr. Sinclair,

We've already discussed the terms of our agreement, and this was not part of that verbal contract. Are you going to take the installment payments or not?

Regards,
Emily Ashworth

His reply arrived within seconds.

Emily,

No. I'm not. The agreement was never solid and is still negotiable. I specifically remember you saying you would do whatever you could to get me what I wanted. That's a pretty broad statement. I wanted

to give you the glasses and contacts as a gift. End
of discussion. I also want you to call me Grady, or
you'll pay later for ignoring my request.

G.

It took Emily several minutes to compose herself, shocked and
amused by his candid response. She couldn't help herself . . . she
answered.

Grady,

How do you plan to make me pay if I call you
Mr. Sinclair?

Emily

His response was immediate this time.

Emily,

Try it and you'll find out.

G.

Oh, Emily was so tempted. Grady was pushing and she wanted to
push back. But sparring with him was dangerous to both her physical
and mental well-being. He fascinated and unsettled her at the same
time.

Her fingers itched to type a reply, but she deleted the e-mails and
closed the page, determined to ignore her attraction to him. She wasn't
used to a man doing anything for her, and she wasn't quite comfortable

with Grady's gift. It was too thoughtful, too insightful. Just the fact that he'd noticed such a small thing about her glasses was perplexing. At the age of twenty-eight, she wasn't a virgin. There had been one boyfriend in college and one after she graduated, but neither of them was anything like Grady Sinclair.

Emily sighed, drew the glasses off her face, and inserted the contact lenses. It was a relief to have clear vision again, and the prescription was perfect. Not that she expected anything less from Grady.

Placing the glasses carefully in her purse, she tried to get back to paperwork, but her mind wandered the rest of the afternoon, day-dreaming about what Grady might do to punish her. Chances were, she'd probably love it.

"I want my truck back," Emily told Grady irritably, stomping her foot in what looked to Grady like a female temper tantrum, but he wasn't entirely sure. Most women he knew just took, and they didn't argue.

Emily had just arrived, toting her suitcase and boxes of red-and-green decorations along with her. She was wearing a Christmas sweatshirt that shouldn't turn him on, but it did. Decked out in Christmas cheer from her tinkling bell earrings to the Christmas socks he could see quite clearly now that she had taken her sneakers off at the door, Grady decided there was one thing he liked about Christmas now—Emily. Even though she was glaring at him, she looked beautiful decked out for the holidays.

In the last two weeks, Grady had felt like he was losing his mind, his only contact with Emily a brief phone discussion about when she'd arrive at his home, communication that had hardly satisfied his need to be close to her. He'd waited for this day for what seemed like forever, and now she was pissed. But he refused to back down, and honestly, he was finding her temper pretty damn adorable and sexy. "No. I already signed the truck over to you." He was handing her the pink slip to his truck, but she was staring at it like it was a snake that was ready to bite her. "Your truck wasn't safe. You've been driving this one for two weeks. If it isn't what you like, I'll get you something else."

"Of course I like it. It's big; it's completely loaded. God, it even has heated leather seats to keep my ass warm. But that isn't the point. It doesn't belong to me. The only reason I've been driving it is because I don't have my truck. You told me we would trade when I got here for Christmas."

"I lied," he answered, not feeling even a tiny bit of guilt. There was no way he was going to give her back an unsafe vehicle to drive. Her hands were propped on her shapely hips, her eyes staring at the paper he was holding out to her, but making absolutely no movement to take it. "Take it. It's one of the things I want," he said, waving the title in front of her face.

"I want my truck. Where is it?" She ignored the paper being held in front of her, and shot him an obstinate look.

Grady didn't think *now* was probably a good time to tell her that her truck was probably in a scrap metal pile somewhere in another city. "It's gone. It was unsafe to drive."

"It was perfectly safe. It just needed new tires. Give it back."

Grady smirked. "Or what? You'll have me arrested for giving you a better truck?"

"You stole my vehicle," she accused, swatting at the hand holding the title to her new ride.

"I replaced a piece of shit with a brand-new truck. It only has a couple hundred miles on it," he told her reasonably.

"Why are you doing this to me?" she asked him, her deep blue eyes confused and vulnerable.

Oh, Christ! Although he liked seeing her all fiery and pissed off, he didn't like her looking *upset*. Those wide blue eyes sucker punched him in the gut, and he quickly tucked the title of the truck into the back pocket of her jeans and scooped her up into his arms.

He sat on the leather couch, bringing her down on top of him. "What did I do? I thought you'd be happy to have a newer vehicle. Yours sucked," he grumbled quietly, watching her angelic face as she stared back at him and tried to scramble off his lap. "Don't move," he demanded, holding her tighter, but not hard enough to hurt her. Having her shapely rear wriggling against his rock-hard cock was torture, but having her warm, cuddly body pressed against him was worth it. "I'm keeping your ass warm," he informed her in what he hoped was a casual voice. "I thought you liked that."

Emily stopped all movement and her head jerked around to look at Grady. A few seconds later, she burst into uncontrollable laughter, her whole body shaking, her eyes tearing with mirth. "This isn't getting you out of giving my truck back, but I can honestly say I've never had someone offer to be my butt warmer before," she gasped, still trying to recover her breath.

"Your truck is nonretrievable. You'll have to take the newer one," Grady answered, knowing that even if he could get it back, he wouldn't. There was no way his woman was driving around in that old hunk of junk during a Maine winter. "Most people would be happy to have a more reliable vehicle." Honestly, he didn't understand her ire. "Why can't you just take it as a Christmas present? You're the one who said Christmas is all about giving. You're not exactly cheery about getting a gift."

"It's too much, Grady," she answered him seriously, her blue eyes warming as she ran her palm along the stubble on his jawline. "I appreciate it, but I can't take a gift that expensive."

He shrugged. "It's not expensive to me. Shouldn't a gift be relative to what someone can afford? I have other vehicles. I even have another truck. I'll never even miss it." It was the truth. He'd gone out and bought another truck right after he'd decided to give her the one she had been driving.

Emily sighed, her eyes searching his face. "We really are from two different worlds. Having that kind of money is unimaginable to me. I have to budget for everything."

"I don't have to budget. I just write a check and I never miss the money. Please take it, Emily. Let me have peace of mind that you're more secure in shitty weather. Please," Grady asked huskily, hoping she'd say yes.

"Do I have a choice?"

"Not really. I think that death trap is probably already scrap metal."

Emily sighed, resigned. "Give me some time, okay? I'm not happy that you made that decision without talking to me first."

Grady shrugged. "You would have said no, and I wouldn't have accepted that. It was easier this way." She might as well get used to it. He was going to protect what was his, and as far as he was concerned, she already belonged to him. He knew she definitely had *him*, whether she wanted him or not.

Dropping her hand, she folded both of them together in her lap, and Grady saw tears begin to stream down her beautiful face.

Fuck!

"I don't know how to deal with this," Emily said, dejected.

"What?" Grady asked, confused.

"I don't understand. I don't know why you're doing this. I'm used to solving my own problems, and I'm not used to having anyone who cares whether I drive an old vehicle or if my glasses are scratched. I'm definitely not accustomed to a man who would donate a million bucks just to spend Christmas with me, thereby saving my ass and maybe my job after another man just used me to get quick access to money." Emily drew a deep breath and added, "I can't figure out your motive and it's driving me crazy. I'm just an ordinary woman. I'm not beautiful or the type of woman any man would lose his mind over. I'm not worth all this, so the things you're doing make absolutely no sense."

Grady had tried to be patient, but as soon as she finished speaking, he completely lost it.

CHAPTER 4

Emily was on her back on the couch, Grady pinning her body to the leather, before she even knew what had happened. Startled, she stared at the fierce expression on his face, looming right above hers, with trepidation. He'd switched positions so fast that her mind was still whirling.

"It's only money. And don't ever say you aren't worth it and that you aren't beautiful," he rumbled angrily. "I grew up with money, I've always had it, and now I have more than I'd need in a hundred lifetimes. I don't give a shit about money. It doesn't make people happy. Rich people can be pretty damn miserable. Maybe it would be worth it to me to actually experience a different kind of Christmas for a change. I think you're worth every stupid thing I give you and a hell of a lot more."

She gaped at him, his words touching a place in her heart that made it ache with sadness. Because right at that moment, she realized that this man *wasn't* happy, and probably never had been. The fact that he hated Christmas should have tipped her off, but she'd been too busy wondering why he was doing anything for her to realize that he was actually hurting. Somewhere deep inside, Grady Sinclair had wounds that weren't visible, but were obviously painful. She'd been too caught up in the money to realize that there was so much more to his behavior than money. In fact, she believed him. The money really did mean nothing to him.

"You don't have to give me anything to spend Christmas with me, Grady. I want to be with you," she answered, feeling the truth in her words. "You didn't need to give so much to the Center, and I don't need an expensive truck. I'm alone this year too," she whispered quietly.

"Not anymore," he answered fiercely. "You have me."

Emily sighed and her body relaxed beneath his. She could have protested that they barely knew each other, that they hadn't had more than a spectacular kiss and a long phone conversation. But, the truth was, she had felt the connection between them from the very moment she'd looked up at him from her undignified position on his front porch. But she was a practical woman, and she was afraid that Grady Sinclair was heartbreak waiting to happen. "Did you really think I was a prostitute? Do you . . . um . . . do that a lot?"

"No. But my younger brother Jared seems to think not getting laid on a regular basis makes me irritable," he replied, his eyes still boring into her, his expression intense.

"Does it?" she asked curiously, wriggling a little to see if she could escape her prison, or at least get her arms loose.

"Not any more irritable than I usually am. But it doesn't stop him from trying occasionally."

Emily's arms finally broke free from between their bodies, and she wrapped them around his neck, aching to try to relieve some of the turmoil she could see in his smoky eyes. "Where is all your family?"

His eyes grew darker. "None of us particularly like the holidays. My father was a drunk, and the holidays weren't a good time for my family. Evan is conveniently on business in another country where they don't celebrate Christmas, and my other brothers are working too. My sister is in Aspen with her latest loser boyfriend whom none of us can talk her into dumping even though all he wants is her money."

"Then I guess you're stuck with me," she told him lightly, stroking the silky strands of hair at the nape of his neck. This man deserved a happier experience, and she was determined to give it to him.

"You're taking the truck," he mumbled stubbornly.

"I'm putting up a Christmas tree," she warned him. "And I'm baking cookies. You have to listen to Christmas music for a whole week."

He grimaced slightly, but answered, "I don't care. As long as you stay, and keep the truck, I'll negotiate." He leaned down and rested his forehead against hers.

Every nerve in Emily's body was vibrating with need, and it was more than just physical. Grady was holding the majority of his weight from her body with his arms, but his muscular body was still plastered against hers from knees to chest, and she could feel the heavy, hard length of his cock pressing against her core. The heat of his body and the scent of his arousal surrounded her, and all she wanted was to melt against him and . . .

Bong. Bong. Bong. Bong. Bong. Bong.

The huge wall clock struck six o'clock, shaking Emily from her sensual thoughts. "Oh shit . . . the party!" She'd been so distracted that she'd completely forgotten that they needed to get to the party at the Center. She wriggled in earnest, knowing she was already late.

Grady sat up, looking like he was extremely reluctant to move. "What party?"

Emily hopped off the couch and to her feet. "The Christmas party at the Center is tonight. I told you I had to be at the annual Christmas party."

"You're not leaving me already?" Grady grumbled, coming to his feet.

"Of course not," she answered excitedly. "You're coming with me."

"I hate parties," he replied with a reluctant expression.

"You won't hate this one," she promised, grabbing his hand and tugging him toward the door. "Most of the town shows up."

"I'm not dressed for a party," he argued.

Emily eyed his jeans and tan cable-knit sweater that looked and felt very much like cashmere. He looked good enough to eat and she'd savor every bite. "It's casual. You look gorgeous."

He shot her a wicked grin that sent incendiary heat directly between her thighs.

Grady Sinclair was an unholy temptation no matter what he was wearing, and she had to tear her gaze away from his to even make it out the door.

Grady went to the party, unable to stop himself from following Emily wherever she led. The woman was like a Pied Piper who led him around by his swollen cock. But the moment they arrived at the YCOA, Emily had to circulate and do her job, so he headed straight for the patio. The guests for the party were already arriving and filling the recreation area of the Center. Wishing he hadn't left his leather jacket at the door, he paced the small patio area to keep warm, reminding himself that he wasn't a kid anymore.

I can do this. I need to do this. If being near Emily means I have to conquer my fears, then damn it, I will.

Striding determinedly toward the glass patio doors that he'd slipped out of earlier, he stepped inside and stopped abruptly, the music and noise hitting him instantly, and his gut started to roil with apprehension.

He could see Emily on the other side of the room, helping Santa pass out gifts to the crowd of children around a massive tree. Some of the adults were dancing on the wooden floor, swaying to a sappy old Christmas tune coming from a set of speakers near the dancing area. Grady suspected that this enormous space was probably a basketball court or a sports area for the kids when it wasn't being used for a Christmas party. Honestly, he didn't have time to look that closely because he was overcome with dizziness and nausea, the floor tilting, his vision blurred as he broke out in a nervous sweat.

Fuck! Not now. I can't do this right now.

Grady's hand grasped the frame of the door to steady himself, cursing his own weakness.

"Grady? Are you okay? Are you sick?" Emily had come over and was standing right in front of Grady.

"Hate parties," he reminded her, his voice graveled and weak.

Emily cupped both sides of his head and tilted his gaze to her. He stared into her gorgeous blue eyes, his vision clearing as she said sternly, "Look at me. Don't look anywhere else. Focus on me."

Her concerned, compassionate, beautiful face turned the world upright again, and his hungry gaze looked at nothing but her. Suddenly, everything else faded, and there was nothing but Emily.

Walking backward, she took his hands and led him into the room, her eyes never leaving his. Grady didn't even notice where she was taking him until she halted at the edge of dance floor.

"I need you to dance with me, Grady. I need you to touch me. Can you do that?" she asked in a sultry, fuck-me-right-now voice.

She needs me.

All Emily had to do was say that she needed him, and he snapped to attention. If she needed, he was going to provide. He wrapped his arms around her with a masculine sigh, his body relaxing as he felt her warm, curvy body mold itself against him, making everything right with the world. Closing his eyes, he inhaled against her temple, the silky strands of her hair caressing his cheek, her warm breath hitting his neck in comforting puffs of air.

"Emily," he mumbled incoherently, every nuance that was uniquely *her* enfolding him as she wrapped her arms around him, stroking his upper back and the nape of his neck. There was no better feeling than holding this woman in his arms. The Christmas music was even louder here, but it didn't matter. He didn't care about the crowd of people he didn't know or what they were thinking. There was only Emily and the way she fit perfectly against his body.

She didn't ask what was wrong; she just held on to him, clung to him, sinking into him like they'd been doing this forever, and Grady savored it. He moved to the rhythm of the music automatically, and Emily followed, the two of them lost in their own little world.

The songs changed, but they still danced, Emily finally tilting her head and whispering to him, "Okay now?"

Grady opened his eyes and looked around him. Some people were looking at him curiously, but mostly all he could see was people genuinely enjoying themselves. The kids were squealing over their presents, showing them off to one another. And the adults were laughing jovially and talking, gathered together in groups around the food tables. Somehow . . . he was able to see everything as an adult, and it was just . . . a party. It was a gathering of people who truly seemed to be having a great time in the company of people they actually *liked*. There wasn't a designer gown or tuxedo anywhere in the room, and these were not the same people who had humiliated him in the past.

"Yeah," he answered gruffly. "Yeah, I am okay." How could he not be absolutely fantastic when he was holding the most gorgeous woman in the room, a woman so warm and sweet that he wanted nothing more than to devour her? "Thanks," he added quietly.

She tilted her head back to look at him with a naughty smile. "No need to thank me. I wanted to dance with the most handsome guy in the room."

Grady grinned. "And you think that's me, huh?"

"I know it is." She winked at him and smiled.

His cock was already hard enough to split diamonds just from holding her. Unable to grow any more engorged, it twitched eagerly, making him swallow a groan. There was nothing he wanted more than to bury himself to the hilt inside Emily and never leave her heat. Dropping his hands to her lower back, he nudged her against him. "I want you so badly I can hardly breathe," he admitted, not caring who heard him.

Her expression turned beautifully aroused, her eyes heated as she glanced back at him longingly. "Kiss me," she demanded breathlessly.

"I'm afraid," Grady answered, falling further under her spell.

"Why?"

"I'm not sure I'll ever be able to stop."

He felt her body trembling, and he couldn't deny her or himself any longer. He swooped down and captured her tempting lips, wanting to brand her as his, make sure she never escaped.

Mine!

The kiss was a declaration for him, a fierce possession to let her know he had no intention of ever letting her go. All pretense of dancing stopped as he threaded his fingers through her hair with one hand, holding her head hostage for his marauding mouth. Then he pressed her hips hard against his groin with his other hand, doing a primal dance that had nothing to do with the holidays.

He demanded, and she gave, submitting herself to his possessive embrace, making him completely lose it.

She's mine.

Grady's need was primitive, and all-consuming, his desire fueled by her submission and passionate response. She clung to him like he was her life raft in the middle of the ocean, and he relished it. All he wanted to do was shelter her, protect her from anything and everything that might harm her, make her smile every single day for the rest of his life.

They broke apart, panting and gasping for breath, staring at each other like they wanted nothing more than to tear each other's clothes off to get closer. Grady nearly groaned at the thought of being skin to skin with her, losing himself in her softness.

I need her so damn much.

He and Emily were in the shadows, but he could see some people looking on with smiles and he heard some wolf whistles, approvals of the show he and Emily had just put on. But he didn't care. Something feral inside him wanted her drenched in his scent, warning every man in the room that she was his.

"I guess not *everyone* thinks I'm the Amesport Beast anymore," he said gutturally, still trying to get his ragged breathing under control.

Emily looked at him, stunned. "You knew people called you that?"

"Of course I knew," he answered hoarsely. "I cultivated the image with my charming personality. As long as people left me alone, I didn't care what they called me."

Emily smacked him on the arm. "I've done everything I can to repair your reputation for the last few weeks. The whole town knows you donated the money to improve the programs here and that you're responsible for us having this party. I thought you were being very unfairly maligned. You were my hero."

Grady liked that thought, and he grimaced at the fact that she had used the past tense in her statement. He wanted to always be her hero, but he shrugged. "I'm not exactly . . . social. I'm an asshole, and all I really had to do was be myself."

Emily sighed and took a breath to respond, but the words never left her lips. Her face suddenly filled with terror as screams began to fill the room and people scrambled. "P-Paul?" Emily stammered, trying to move out of Grady's arms. "What are you doing?"

Grady's gaze shot to a man standing about ten feet to the side of them, a handgun aimed directly at Emily's head. The guy was wavering, his hands shaking as he held his arms straight in front of him, the lethal weapon slightly tilted. A lunatic, cold, and lifeless gaze trained on Emily told Grady several things at a quick glance: the man was drunk or high, desperate, and determined to die.

Oh, fuck no! He'd just found Emily, and he wasn't losing her. The bastard could go screw himself. Shifting their positions, he shielded Emily with his body. He could feel her resistance, but she was no match for his brute strength and the adrenaline pumping through his body. The asshole would have to go through him to get to her.

"This your new boyfriend, Emily?" the gunman asked, taking a few steps closer and waving the gun toward Grady. "Grady Sinclair, the billionaire genius. Did you know he's had agents on my ass for two weeks? Everywhere I go, at every one of my usual hiding places, my friends tell me that Grady Sinclair has had his private security force there looking for me. I've had to hide like a rabbit, in some of the dirtiest holes imaginable, because I can't stay in my usual hideouts. The police never would have found me without you and your boyfriend's help. He put private investigators everywhere, and they report everything to the police. There's nowhere left for me to hide anymore. This place is going to be surrounded in a few minutes and I'm not going to prison because his employees are breathing down my neck now along with the police. I'd rather die. But I'm taking you and your asshole boyfriend with me," Paul said, his voice high, desperate, and slurred. "The police never would have found me without his money and power to put so many people on my ass that I couldn't escape."

"Paul, don't do this. You don't need to shoot anyone," Emily cried, panicked. "We can walk out of here right now. I'll go with you as a hostage so you can get away—as long as you don't use the gun."

Grady gritted his teeth, his jaw tight, turning her farther toward safety while his eyes never left the dull, dead eyes of the criminal beside him. His arm gripped like a steel band around Emily's waist. "Over my dead body," he growled loud enough for her to hear him.

The bastard might take her, but he'd kill her. Grady could tell by the look on the man's face that he was determined to die and would be more than happy to take him, Emily, and anyone else who got in his way, along with him. In fact, that was exactly what he wanted. The guy had obviously snapped, his sanity gone. The gun that was swaying in Paul's hand was a Beretta semiautomatic, and Grady shuddered at the number of kids in the building. Luckily, people were pouring out the front door, taking their children out of danger. "Get ready to run like hell and don't look back," Grady ordered Emily in a harsh whisper, mentally wishing everyone would hurry the fuck up and get outside. But not everyone was leaving. There were men in the building who had taken cover, but it was mostly the women and children who were exiting. The men were staying as backup, but sending their women and kids out of harm's way.

"Close those doors. Nobody else leaves," Paul screamed in a high-pitched voice.

Go. Go. Go. Grady could see the last of the women stream out the door with the kids, the door slamming shut behind them.

And then there was silence.

The only thing he could hear was his heart thundering in his ears, his rage at the fact that Emily was still in danger barely leashed. Grady's eyes narrowed as Paul stepped closer, now about five feet from his woman. He watched as the gunman's finger started to twitch on the trigger, the wail of sirens making him edgy. Gut instinct was making the call for Grady, and he knew the time was *now*.

"Run!" he demanded urgently, blocking Emily with his entire body as he lunged for Paul.

The gun fired once as Grady took the asshole down, but it discharged as the two of them were falling, and he took solace in the fact that Emily should be long gone. Finally, Grady let go of the rage that had been simmering inside of him, tearing the gun from Paul's hand and sliding it far across the wooden floor for one of the other men to retrieve. He was seeing red, his entire focus on the man who had hurt his woman and put her in danger again tonight.

"You'll never hurt her again," he growled, slamming Paul's head against the hardwood floor.

Crack!

The sound of the bastard's skull hitting the floor was so satisfying that Grady never felt the punches Paul was giving back as Grady pummeled him, not wanting to stop until any threat to Emily was gone, the man beneath him dead.

Several uniformed officers came between them, two pulling Grady off the battered gunman and two more rolling Paul over to cuff him.

"Easy, man. Let us take over," one of the officers told him as they laid Grady on his back. "You've been shot." The police started holding pressure to Grady's side, his expression somber. Raising his head slightly, Grady could see blood. Lots of blood. He wished it had come from the asshole the police were carting away, but he knew it hadn't. It was his, and he was finally coming out of his haze enough to feel the pain from the wound.

"Oh, God," Grady heard Emily cry out as she dropped to her knees beside him, handing a policeman the weapon she had obviously recovered when he had slid it across the floor. "Grady! Talk to me, love."

"I told you to run. Don't you listen? Are you hurt?"

"No. And I wasn't leaving you. I wanted to shoot him, but I was afraid I'd hit you," she replied, her voice tremulous and scared, making Grady wish he could beat the shit out of Paul all over again.

If Grady weren't so pissed that she hadn't taken herself out of harm's way, he would have been more touched that she'd been so worried about him that she hadn't run away. "Could you try listening when I'm trying to keep you safe? Stubborn woman," he grumbled, flinching as the cop applied a little more pressure to his wound.

Emily took his hand and threaded her fingers through his, stroking his hair back from his forehead. "What am I going to do with you?" she asked, forlorn.

"Keep me," he answered, his vision starting to blur. "And don't give me any more hassle about the new truck." Okay . . . he was taking advantage, but he'd use every bit of leverage he could get at the moment.

"You're going to use the edge you have right now to get me to agree?" she asked hesitantly.

"Yep." He was using whatever he could get.

"Okay," she whispered agreeably. "If it will make you happy, I'll do it. Whatever you want right now."

It made him fucking ecstatic, or as joyful as a guy could be who had just gotten shot. He felt her lips on his forehead right before everything started to fade to black, and decided right then and there that being fussed over by Emily wasn't a bad way to go out.

CHAPTER 5

Emily decided almost immediately that Grady Sinclair was probably the worst patient to ever enter their small-town hospital. He'd wanted to leave the minute the doctor had sutured the gaping wound in his side. Luckily, the bullet had just grazed his flesh, but it had left a substantial laceration.

She had cried like a blubbering child when the doctor had said Grady would be okay with some suturing, antibiotics, and an overnight stay for observation. It might have been amusing that Grady had actually been trying to comfort her when he was the one in pain.

It had been her fault—Paul was *her* crazy ex-boyfriend—but Grady had risked his own life to save her anyway. Honestly, Emily didn't think he had even given a thought to his own safety. He had only cared about hers, and the fact that he'd been willing to sacrifice his life to protect her completely floored her. No man she'd ever known, except maybe her father, would have protected her without a single thought to his own safety. Now she was determined to take care of Grady.

Keeping him in the hospital had been a challenge, and she had gotten desperate and threatened to break her promise to spend Christmas with him if he didn't follow the doctor's orders. He grumbled and protested, but he had finally given in. He'd gotten even grouchier when she refused to leave him, telling her to take her ass home and get some sleep. She slept in the recliner beside his bed, not only because she wanted to be with him in case he needed anything, but because she was afraid he'd get up and leave if she didn't keep him in the bed.

Emily breathed a sigh of relief as she got him back home the next afternoon, more than ready to be away from the hospital and the thoughts that kept racing through her mind about what could have happened to Grady.

"You didn't tell me you got a tree!" Emily exclaimed as they entered the house, noticing the huge Christmas tree in the corner of the living room. It was a beauty, full and lush, and at least seven feet tall.

"You like it?" he asked cautiously, grimacing as he moved. "You said you wanted one. I asked the lady who cleans the house where I could get a big one. She said she'd have her husband bring one here and set it up. I guess they brought it this morning."

"You're hurting. Do you want some pain medicine?" she asked him anxiously.

"No. Do you like the tree?"

"It's beautiful. I'll decorate it later. Right now I just want to get you to bed." She wrapped her arm around his waist, careful not to put pressure on his wound.

"Sweetheart, those are words I've wanted to hear from you since the moment I met you. And I'm not going to bed unless you come with me," he replied obstinately, raising a teasing brow at her as he added, "Seriously? Do you really think you're going to hold me up if I swoon?"

"Yes. I'm stronger than I look," she told him defensively. Okay . . . maybe she couldn't hold him up, but she could make his trip to the ground less painful.

"Not that I'm complaining, mind you. Feel free to get as close as you want to get," he told her playfully as he moved slowly toward the stairs.

Emily walked him up the staircase, staying close to him because she needed to be there. She followed him to his bedroom, ready to put him into the enormous bed that looked incredibly inviting.

"Bed," she insisted.

"Shower," he said gruffly. "Are you planning to come with me? I could fall and hit my head. Or I might get dizzy."

She had to bite her lip to keep from smiling. She had no doubt Grady was in pain, but he was playing this for all it was worth. "I'll wait outside the door."

"But what if I need you?" he argued with a weak but wicked grin.

"I'll be close," she said sternly, her hands lifting to start unbuttoning his shirt, knowing the motion to do it himself would be painful for him.

"Not close enough," he said hoarsely. "It's going to take me a while to get the image of that asshole pointing a gun at your head to go away."

Unfastening the last button, she opened his shirt and had to force herself not to gape at the mouthwatering sight of his bare chest and ripped abdomen; his smooth, warm skin stretched over sculpted muscle had her struggling not to salivate.

I need to be clinical. I have to help him. Grady needs me.

She slipped the shirt over his shoulders and let it drop to the floor. "Um . . . can you handle it from here?" She gulped, looking at the jeans sitting low on his hips, and the fine trail of hair that ran down into the waistband of his jeans. The man had a body that would tempt a saint, and she certainly wasn't that angelic.

"Nope. Movement hurts. You'll have to do it," he said, deadpan.

Her eyes shot to his face. His expression was stoic, but his eyes were pure wicked heat. Her nipples hardened, and fire slithered from her belly and came to rest between her thighs. Even injured, Grady Sinclair was all masculine temptation for her, an alluring mix of demanding male and boyish mischief who had her wondering if she should laugh or be completely mortified.

"Grady," she warned, licking her parched lips as she looked up at him.

"I need your help, Emily. Please."

She couldn't deny him, and to be honest, she couldn't resist the opportunity to touch him. Her hands were trembling as she reached for the button of his jeans, grateful that there was only one button with a zipper. Honestly, she knew this task would hurt him, the movement required to shower probably excruciating. The arm movements required would pull at his sutures, and the last thing she wanted was for him to reinjure himself. He might be challenging her, but she was knee-deep in this task because she couldn't stand to cause him another moment of pain.

Her decision made, she pushed him toward the master bath that she had seen as they entered the bedroom. His face flashed a moment of surprise and great deal of longing as he moved obediently.

Once in the bathroom, she lowered the zipper down on his jeans, unable to keep from noticing that she had to work around a very large and hard appendage as she started pulling them down and off his hips, taking a pair of silky boxers along with the pants. "You're going to let me do all the work. You stand there and let me help you," she demanded as she motioned for him to step out of his pants now that they were down to his knees.

Before she could think about it and change her mind, she whipped her sweatshirt over her head and let it fall to the floor. Her jeans followed, leaving her feeling completely exposed in only a skimpy bra and panties. After seeing his body, she tried not to fidget with discomfort as she felt his gaze on her. She was body conscious and not particularly fond of parading around almost nude. But right now, her insecurities weren't as important as Grady.

The shower was fancy, and she had to fiddle with the various controls to get the settings correct, but she managed. Holding open the door of the enclosure, she motioned to a naked Grady. "Get in." His wound was already covered in a protective waterproof bandage, but she'd have to be careful.

He didn't move, his eyes roaming over her body and filled with desire. "God, you're so beautiful it hurts to look at you."

Emily reached up, pulled the clip from her hair, and let the locks fall haphazardly to her shoulders.

She heard Grady groan, and she knew it wasn't from pain. He really did find her attractive and nearly irresistible. Feminine power surged through her body, her insecurities falling away as she looked at his fierce eyes caressing her body like she was the only woman alive. And, God, it was intoxicating.

"Get in the shower, Grady," she told him forcefully, knowing she needed a moment to get her thoughts together. "I have to take out my contacts."

It was the break she needed. She dashed down the staircase in her underwear and grabbed her suitcase, bringing it back upstairs with her so she could get her lens case. Her hands shook as she removed her lenses and placed them in the plastic container, taking deep breaths and trying to remind herself that she was taking care of Grady. He needed her right now.

Stepping back into a bathroom that was now foggy with steam, she heard a groan from the shower and yanked the door open. "I told you not to move," she scolded, completely forgetting anything else except her need to keep Grady from hurting himself. She snatched the soapy sponge from his hand and dropped it to the shower floor. Reaching for his masculine-smelling soap, she lathered her hands and started stroking his body with long, languid motions, starting with his back, massaging the tense muscles as she worked.

Every inch of Grady's body was solid muscle, and as she moved down to his ass, she could feel the incredibly toned glutes that she'd only admired from afar and covered by denim. They were so much hotter and so very real beneath her fingertips, flexing as she smoothed the soap over them.

Get him clean and into bed.

Finishing the back of his body, she washed his hair, pushing his head forward to rinse. "Turn," she instructed quietly.

He turned compliantly, and she started on his front, nearly moaning as she stroked over the sculpted muscles of his chest.

"Strip," Grady said huskily. "I want you naked right now. If I can't fuck you, I at least want to see you."

"I'm washing you. I don't need to finish undressing—"

"Take it all off or I'll do it," he warned dangerously.

Emily knew he'd do it, and he'd hurt himself. Really, did it matter? She was nearly naked anyway.

She set the soap on the ledge and unhooked the front catch of her bra, pulling the soaked garment off her body. Her panties went down her legs easily, her hands still slick with soap. "I'll smell like you," she told him jokingly, feeling suddenly vulnerable before him. Wringing out the lingerie, she hung them over the door.

"Good. I want my scent all over you." He reached out and pulled her against his body, stroking his hand over her back and down, his strong fingers cupping her ass and bringing her aching core against his engorged cock. He moved forward and pinned her body between the tile wall of the enclosure and his overwhelmingly masculine form. "I want you underneath me, moaning my name while I bury myself inside you. I want to watch you come," he said harshly, his breath coming hard and fast.

"Don't!" Emily cried, the sound half worry and half longing. "You'll hurt yourself." She pushed lightly on his chest, trying to get him to release her.

"Then I suggest you don't move," he answered in a hoarse, tortured whisper. "Because I have to touch you. I need to touch you. The pain of not touching you is killing me."

Emily released a tremulous breath, staying still as he backed up slightly, their eyes meeting and holding. His were filled with a fierce, covetous need that made her entire body quiver and burn like an inferno. Desire clawed at her, some unknown force locking and fusing them together, making her crave him, wanting him to take her in the most carnal ways possible.

His hands moved over her body, while his gaze stayed locked with hers. He cupped her breasts and his thumbs circled and stroked her nipples into hard, sensitive peaks. It was as if the caress of his fingers fired every nerve ending in her body, making her rock her hips, moaning softly as her whole body trembled. She bit her lip, trying to hold back her pleasure, but it wouldn't be contained.

Grady took his time, exploring the valley between her breasts as one of his hands moved lower, his fingers moving in erotic circles on her sensitized flesh.

"I want to be fucking you right now, but I'll settle for this." His hand moved between her thighs, his fingers delving slowly between her wet folds. "I'll watch you come."

Emily's hands slapped against the tile, her knees weakening as Grady explored leisurely, his fingers stroking from her anus to her clit, over and over again. Each time, his finger barely brushed the tiny bundle of nerves, the bud engorged and needy. Her moan escaped her lips completely, and she whimpered, "Please."

His eyes were blazing with liquid heat as he finally moved his thumb over her clit, but the pressure wasn't enough. Emily's eyes fluttered closed, and she thrust her hips forward, begging for relief from the erotic torture. He rotated from breast to breast with his other hand, pinching her nipple hard enough to send a jolt of electric pulsation through her body, followed by a smooth caress.

"Tell me what you want, sweetheart," he demanded, his heated breath caressing her neck, his mouth close to her ear. "Tell me."

"You," she moaned, her chest heaving as Grady finally moved his fingers over her clit with more pressure, more urgency.

His mouth covered hers, stealing her breath as his tongue invaded, taking away any will of her own. She was consumed by Grady, and he was stoking her body to a fevered state that left her helpless to his marauding tongue and his demanding fingers.

Over and over, his fingers rubbed over her clit, every brush taking her higher. His tongue was mimicking what he'd like to do with his cock, thrusting in and out of her mouth like a man possessed.

Finally, Emily couldn't take it anymore. She moved her hand down to cover his, desperate for a rough, vigorous touch that would send her over the edge.

He was panting as his mouth came away from hers. "Open your eyes. Tell me what you want."

"You know what I want," she gasped, entwining her fingers with his and pushing his fingers against her clit harder, faster.

"Open your eyes. I want to watch you come," he rasped. "Tell me that's what you want."

"Make me come. Please," she pleaded, opening her eyes to meet his feral expression.

He looked satisfied with her answer, and finally gave her what she needed so desperately. Grasping her hand with his, he moved their entwined fingers with bold strokes that had her panting and gasping. "Come for me, angel. Now."

Emily couldn't have held back if she tried. It was as if he knew exactly what would send her over the edge, and she felt her impending climax clawing at her belly as the pulsation began. Letting out a long moan, she tilted her head back, her eyes never breaking contact with Grady's fierce, possessive, and determined stare.

"Oh, God," she choked out as the climax thrummed through her body, her entire being shaken by an orgasm so intense that she had to reach for the handle on the door of the shower to keep herself on her feet.

Grady held her, keeping her steady as he kissed her tenderly, as though he were tasting the last drop of her pleasure, absorbing the last of her ecstasy.

Emily floated down slowly, Grady pulling her close and rocking her body against his as she recovered. She shivered, and he turned her so the hot water was at her back, and that small protective gesture just put her under his spell a little deeper.

"Are you okay?" she asked, worried that he'd strained something. She'd tried to be still, but it was more movement than he should be doing at the moment.

"I just lived a fantasy. I'm better than okay," he answered, amusement in his voice.

It wasn't most men's fantasy to watch a woman orgasm without having one of their own, but this was Grady, and he was the most unselfish man she'd ever known. The fact that fulfilling her needs was his fantasy made her want to cry for some strange reason. Maybe because he was the first man who ever really gave a shit about making her happy? Her hand slid down his sculpted abdomen and curled around his rigid cock. He was rock hard, and Emily could almost feel the blood throbbing through the shaft.

Grady groaned and moved his hand down to take her fingers away from him. "I can't take much more, angel."

"Let me. Please," she begged, needing to make him feel as good as he had made her feel. "But you have to stay very still," she teased. "No hurting yourself."

"Baby, I already hurt, but not from the damn sutures. I want to be deep inside you right now. I want to be buried in you, in your heat, until I burn."

Stepping back, she ran her hand down his chest, savoring the flex of muscle beneath her fingers. "You'll have to settle for this," she told him in a sultry voice as she followed her hand and dropped to her knees on the tile.

"Emily. No," he said in a husky, tortured groan.

Her hand continued to stroke up and down the shaft as her tongue flicked out to lick the velvety head. "No?" she questioned.

"Oh, fuck yeah," he panted harshly.

Smiling, she took him into her mouth and did one long suck, bringing a strangled groan from Grady as she repeated it again. She moved her tongue down his long length, and then took as much of him as she could manage. Her hands moved, needing to touch his body, finally settling her palms on his ass and gripping it hard as she devoured him.

"Fuck. Fuck. Fuck," he groaned. "That feels so damn good. I won't last."

His hips thrust, and one of his hands came down to thread through her soaking-wet hair, guiding her head as she opened her jaw as wide as she could, trying to take his cock deeper. Her throat squeezed tight with every entry, massaging the front of his shaft, bringing a strangled groan from Grady with every thrust. Her fingernails dug into his tight ass, pulling him to her with every stroke.

"Sweetheart . . . Fuck . . . I can't . . . I'll come in your mouth," he growled incoherently.

That was exactly what she wanted. She wanted to taste him, and her hunger for him was ferocious. Sucking harder and faster, she felt him shudder before his hot release flooded the back of her throat, flowing warmly into her as he gasped, threw his head back, and released a satisfying groan of ecstasy.

He tasted tangy, slightly salty, and so completely like Grady.

She protested when he hauled her up before she could get to her feet, not wanting him to lift anything. He brushed off her concern and kissed her passionately, and then pulled her against his chest. He rocked her again, just like he'd done when she'd climaxed.

Emily didn't know how long they stayed wrapped together, their bodies humming and their souls singing. All she knew was a feeling of total happiness, and the sense that in Grady's embrace, she was exactly where she needed to be. She thought she had come home to Amesport, but with Grady, Emily felt like she had finally found her real home.

CHAPTER 6

"Do you want to tell me what happened to you at the party?" Emily asked quietly in the dark, her body spooned with Grady in his huge bed.

"I got shot," he answered gravely, his baritone vibrating against her ear.

She knew that he was hedging. He knew exactly what she was talking about. "Before that. Your panic attack," she said patiently.

"I don't like parties," he said hesitantly, stroking his hand along her hip absently.

"It's more than that. But if you don't want to share it with me, it's okay," she told him softly.

She might have ended up going to business school for her MBA, but she'd done her undergrad work in psychology. She recognized social anxiety when she saw it.

"It isn't that I don't want to share everything with you. I'm just not really sure how to explain it," he admitted reluctantly, letting out a long, masculine sigh. "When I was young, I stuttered pretty badly."

"Lots of kids do. And you obviously outgrew it." But she knew it probably hadn't been easy. "Kids can be brutal sometimes. They teased you?"

"Yeah. But it wasn't so much the teasing at school. It was at home."

"Your siblings?" she asked, confused.

"My father," Grady said, his voice rough. "I was a Sinclair, and no Sinclair is supposed to have any defect. I could never get my words out, and my father thought I was stupid. He never let a day go by without reminding me that I wasn't the son he wanted. I was supposed to be social, one of the Sinclair elite. I wasn't. I was a computer geek. I didn't really like business. And I had no desire to play the socialite games. None of it was real."

Emily's heart felt like it was in a vise, seeing visions of a young Grady feeling like he never measured up to his father's rigorous standards. "But you're a genius," she argued. "Look at all you've accomplished."

"Didn't matter. I wasn't like him. And he didn't think I was smart. He thought I was defective. Even though I did eventually outgrow my stuttering, he never saw me as anything but an idiot."

Not sure if she wanted to know, she asked hesitantly, "And the party thing?"

"We had the Sinclair annual Christmas party every year, an event that every Sinclair had to attend. My father was an alcoholic, and he got even more verbally abusive when he was drinking. Since he couldn't claim me or accept me as his son, he did his best to humiliate me every year, showing all of his rich friends that he shunned me, making me the family joke. And almost every one of them went along with it, laughed it up with him about me being the Sinclair moron. I guess it's okay to have one of *those*, but he couldn't exactly claim me as part of *his* family. I was nothing to be proud of." Taking a deep breath, he finished, "I was always . . . different."

"I'm glad you're different. It's better than being a carbon copy of a mean drunk," Emily said fiercely. "No wonder you learned to dread Christmas. Did you celebrate at all as a family?"

"Only the party," Grady admitted. "We were Sinclairs," he said, as though that explained everything. "We decorated because of the party."

"Where are your parents now?" she asked, wondering if she could strangle his father for putting those kinds of fears and insecurities into an innocent boy.

"My father is dead. He passed away right after the Christmas party when I was eighteen. My mother remarried and moved to Europe. We almost never see her. I think we were a part of her life that she wanted to forget. I don't think she was ever happy," Grady mused.

Emily breathed a sigh of relief. She didn't want to commit murder, and if she were in the same room as his alcoholic father, she might have been tempted. "Are you close to your siblings?"

"As close as we can be considering we're never together," he answered quietly.

She had a feeling they had all suffered from being brought up in a home with very little love and an alcoholic father with a short fuse. "How did you ever turn out so special?" she queried softly.

"You mean different?" he asked, confused.

"No . . . special. Extraordinary. Incredible."

"You think I am? I'm odd," Grady said nonchalantly.

"You are not odd. You donated a ridiculous amount of money to the Center when a much smaller amount would have saved it. I know you won't admit it, but you care about the programs there. You're the kind of man who sends Lord knows how many men out just to find one man who stole from a charity. You made the effort to get me a Christmas tree even though you don't like Christmas. You're incredible," Emily answered emphatically. "And don't you ever say you aren't. You're the most unique man I've ever known."

"Is that good or bad?" he questioned, sounding slightly amused. "'Unique' sort of sounds the same as 'different.'"

"It's not. And I think you're wonderful," she answered decisively. "You are special, Grady. You just don't see it. You're brilliant, kind, giving—"

"Ornery, antisocial, irritating, and the Amesport Beast?" he added.

"None of us is perfect, and the only reason people said that is because they didn't know you," Emily answered with a delighted laugh. "I'm afraid you're going to have to live with your good deeds now because you're the local hero."

"I only care about you. I want to be your hero," he answered hopefully.

She turned carefully, trying not to put any pressure on his wound. Wrapping her arms around his neck, she stroked his hair, her heart flip-flopping as she rested her cheek against his rough jaw. Grady was so much more than her hero. He was becoming her everything, but she simply answered, "You are. Believe me . . . you definitely are. You probably saved my life." She kissed him lightly on the forehead, wishing she could take away the pain of his childhood. She couldn't, but she could try to teach him that his past didn't have to define his future.

"You know the old Chinese proverb . . . If you save someone's life, you're responsible for it forever," he answered contentedly.

"Don't worry. I won't hold you to that," she commented lightly.

"I want you to hold me to it. Forever," he said sleepily, wrapping his arm around her waist just a little bit tighter.

Emily wasn't quite sure how to respond. Her heart skipped a beat, but she didn't want to read too much into what he said. He was hurt, exhausted, and under the influence of the pain pill he had taken before they'd crawled into bed.

It's better if I don't say anything. Then I won't get hurt. Again.

It was cowardly, and she knew it, but everything was so real and so incredibly intense with Grady. She wanted to be prepared, because the pain of losing the fragile relationship they were forming would probably kill her.

Exhausted, they fell into silence, and finally slept.

Grady discovered quite a few new things about Emily Ashworth over the next several days. He learned that she loved Christmas carols, and she sang along with them completely out of tune. But her enthusiasm made up for her being a little off-key, so he found it pretty adorable. Her Christmas cookies were out of this world, and she couldn't make them fast enough to keep any around for long. She'd tried to hide some, but Grady had managed to ferret them out almost immediately, sneaking into the kitchen when she wasn't looking and wolfing them down like he'd never had Christmas cookies before. He had . . . years ago . . . but they hadn't been anywhere near as good as Emily's. He'd also learned she cried over Christmas movies that were her old favorites. She professed to love them, but they made her cry. What she called "happy tears" weren't really something he was familiar with. Why would someone cry when they were happy?

The laceration on his side was healing, but not quickly enough. Grady relived that first night in the shower with Emily over and over in his mind, his need to bury himself inside her and claim her nearly an obsession. He walked around with a constant erection, but Emily refused to let him do anything she considered physical, so he was in a continual state of frustrated lust.

Still, they were the happiest days he could remember. Doing the simplest of things with Emily was special. And the more time she spent in his house and in his life, the more he knew he was never letting her go. He couldn't even think about not having her with him anymore. He thought of her as his own Christmas angel. And she had landed on *his* doorstep.

Mine!

She was his . . . she just hadn't realized it yet. Hell, she even had him loving Christmas. It was now his favorite holiday, the memories of the past being obliterated by Emily and all the things she did just for the joy of doing them, never expecting anything in return.

Grady lifted his eyes from his computer for a moment to watch Emily, sitting on the floor of his office, sorting out boxes of paperwork. In a pair of worn jeans and a bright red sweater, she was absolutely mesmerizing. With Emily, it wasn't one single feature or personality trait that drew him . . . It was the entire package. There wasn't one single thing about her that didn't have him completely fascinated. Okay . . . her stubbornness drove him crazy occasionally, but even the annoyed looks she gave him were pretty damn cute. He watched her face as various emotions changed her expressions: irritation, confusion, concentration, and finally elation when she figured something out.

He had to clench his fists on the desk to keep himself from getting out of his chair behind his desk and taking her right there on the floor. He'd had a small taste of her sweetness, but it wasn't enough. And she'd refused to let him get any more than a kiss since that afternoon, her fear of him hurting himself making her back away every time. There was no sweeter sound than the arousing little noises and moans that escaped from her lips when she was climaxing. Watching her had been the most satisfying experience of his life, and he wanted to see her face when he was deep inside her heat, losing himself in her softness while he pounded her into orgasm.

Grady wasn't sure how much longer he could wait. Watching her like this was torture, and work was impossible, although he was trying to get some stuff done on his current project. If she was close, he wanted to watch her. If she wasn't, he wanted to seek her out. He was pretty much screwed either way.

"How can a billionaire possibly be so disorganized?" she said distractedly, sifting through another box of papers, her brows drawn together in disapproval. "And why do you create these awesome businesses just to sell them off?"

Grady smiled, knowing his filing system drove her crazy—basically because he didn't have one. "I like creating them, but I don't like managing them. Once I'm done putting everything together, I'm ready to start another project."

She glanced up at him with a frown. "But every business you've started has gone on to be a huge Internet sensation."

Grady shrugged. "I get paid well for them. I'm not social, and I don't interact with people all that well."

"What are you working on now?" she asked curiously, pulling another pile of papers out of a box and setting them on her lap. She was determined to organize him.

With his history and personality, it probably wouldn't make sense to her at all, but he answered, "A new social media site."

She was silent for a moment as she stared at him, probably trying to figure out if he was really serious. "Why?" she asked hesitantly.

Grady shrugged. "Because I can, I guess. Those who don't socialize develop social media sites for others who do."

She looked at him incredulously, and then burst into laughter, her delighted shrieks echoing in the large room. "Oh, Grady, you're brilliant. And your communication is fine. You just never let anyone really know you. Is there anything you can't do?" She was still holding her stomach and gasping for breath from her fits of laughter.

Get you to let me fuck you.

The one thing he wanted, he couldn't seem to accomplish. Aloud, he said, "I obviously can't file."

"I don't think that it's a matter of not being capable—you obviously just don't want to do it," she answered, her skeptical look challenging him.

Busted!

"Paperwork is boring and tedious," he answered defensively.

"So what . . . you build an online business with your genius, sell it off, and just throw the contracts and everything else into a box when you're done?"

Grady fidgeted uncomfortably, 'cause really, she was pretty damn close to the truth. "Of course not," he said irritably. *I also deposit the check, or get the wire transfer into my bank.*

"Grady Sinclair, I can follow your last five years of work from the mess in these boxes," she told him ominously. "But none of it is organized."

"The tax stuff is all in the computer," he argued, beginning to enjoy himself. Obviously, his record keeping offended her ultraorganized MBA personality.

"Do you even know how much money you have right now?"

Grady smirked. "A lot." He had a financial manager who kept him on top of things, but he honestly didn't know the exact balance of his accounts every single day. That was why he paid the best in the business to do it for him. "I look occasionally and the balances are always going up, so that's good, right?" Okay . . . he was yanking her chain a bit, but he loved to watch her reactions.

Emily threw her hands in the air in frustration. "But what if it's not invested properly? What if you could be doing better . . . but you aren't . . . because you aren't watching things?"

God, he loved watching her stubborn, protective look. Emily was trying to watch out for *him*, and his heart soared. But the worried look on her face got to him. He got up and walked to where she was sitting and picked up the laptop computer next to her. Holding the computer with one hand, he logged in to a website and handed the computer to her. "My portfolio is fine. See for yourself."

She took the computer from him and stretched her legs out, propping it on her thighs.

He walked back to the desk and sat back down in his chair, watching her face as she flipped from one page to the next, her brows wrinkled in concentration. Smiling, he propped his feet on his desk and crossed his hands over his abdomen. Watching Emily had become his favorite activity. "Happy now?" he asked, after watching her analyze everything for several minutes, catching on to the workings of the portfolio tracker site very quickly. "Do you think my financial manager is doing a good job?"

"He's more than good," she said, her voice dripping with admiration. "He's incredible. Who is he?" Her head was still down, her complete focus on the numbers.

"Jason Sutherland," he answered, disgruntled, and not quite sure he liked the reverent expression on her face as he said Jason's name.

"*The* Jason Sutherland?" she asked, her tone reaching the point of awe.

Grady nodded abruptly, now certain he hated Jason.

"My idol," she sighed, setting the computer to the side as she looked up at him. "He's incredible."

"He's not that great," Grady grumbled, knowing he was lying. Jason was one of the most intelligent men he knew, but he wasn't going to admit it when Emily had that dreamy look on her face.

"He doesn't do personal portfolios. He doesn't need to. He's already worth billions, the golden boy genius of the investment world. I know you're a wealthy man. Um . . . okay . . . really wealthy, but he doesn't do portfolios for anyone but himself. He was already incredibly wealthy when I was in business school. I used to study his investment strategies. And he's so young."

"The same age as me," Grady answered, wanting to not talk about Jason anymore. Emily looked too enthralled, and it was irritating him.

"How do you know him?"

"He's my friend. I've known him since childhood," he grumbled. "I suppose you think he's gorgeous too?" Most women did, and the female adoration Jason got had never bothered Grady before, but it bugged the hell out of him now.

"Nope. I've never met him, of course, but I don't think he looked the least bit attractive in his pictures. But he's incredibly good with investments," she answered, rising to her feet.

"You don't think he's hot?" Grady questioned, his voice full of disbelief.

"No," she answered quietly, her hips swaying as she moved closer to Grady. "He's too pretty, almost too perfect. I much prefer tall, dark beasts who make generous donations to charities and aren't obsessed with their money." She bent over and kissed him softly, lingering just long enough to make Grady nearly insane.

Her scent enveloped him, and her lips tasted like sweet coffee and sin.

She moved back slowly and rested her forehead against his. "I'm on to you, Grady Sinclair. You donate millions to charity. I thought your donation to the Center was incredible, but you do that all the time, don't you? I saw some of the receipts, and I have a feeling there are a lot more I haven't seen yet."

Grady shrugged and swallowed hard before answering. "I don't need the money. They're all good causes."

"I find men who donate millions quietly to charities without wanting people to know how generous they really are incredibly hot," she said in a husky whisper.

Right at that moment, Grady wanted to donate most of his fortune to charity so Emily would find him even hotter. *Christ!* If he didn't get inside this woman very shortly, he was going to spontaneously combust.

Mine!

"Did you actually think I was hot for your friend? Were you . . . jealous?" she asked slowly, as though she didn't believe it was possible.

"Yes," he answered immediately. "He might be my friend, but I wanted to tear his head off because I thought you wanted him. Does that scare you?" Honestly, it kind of scared the hell out of him.

I'm losing my fucking mind. I like Jason. He's a good guy. But one mention from Emily that she admired him, and I'm ready to lose it.

"No. I've just never had a guy who wanted me that much," she answered in a tremulous voice.

"I do," he growled, grabbing her around the waist and swinging her onto his lap.

"Careful," she scolded, trying to wriggle off his lap. "You still aren't healed. Let me up."

He wanted to tell her she was healing him, and his gunshot injury was doing fine too. "Kiss me first," he demanded, spearing a hand through her hair, but waiting for her to kiss him because she wanted to be as close to him as he wanted to be to her.

"I don't want to hurt you," she said nervously.

"Then you damn well better hurry up and kiss me, or I'm going to expire right here in this chair." Shit, he was desperate, and he needed some connection to her right now. His cock was trying to burst out of his jeans, and he knew she could feel it cuddling up to her ass. "Stay here and let me keep your ass warm," he told her gruffly, putting mild pressure on the back of her head. "Kiss me."

Emily nibbled on her lip, as though she were considering the risks and benefits. "Are you sure you're okay?"

"I'm dying," he rumbled. "Kiss me or kill me."

Emily giggled and boldly lowered her mouth to his.

CHAPTER 7

I'm in love with Grady Sinclair.

Emily knew how she felt about Grady with a certainty that was frightening. There was no wondering if it was true, or any indecision about if that love was the real thing. They'd known each other for such a short time, but he'd had her from the moment he'd helped her up from his porch and cleaned off her glasses for her without a second thought. He'd snatched her heart with that one insignificant but thoughtful gesture, and she'd fallen deeper and deeper as every piece of Grady's puzzling personality fell into place.

Really, he wasn't such a great mystery. He was a man who followed his conscience, led his life the way he needed to for his own happiness, and gave to others because he wanted to do it. And he was lonely, not because he wanted to be alone, but because he was afraid he'd never be accepted. He'd felt different all his life.

It made Emily want to give *him* everything he needed, but she was afraid. If she gave everything over to Grady and things didn't work out, there would be nothing left, no pieces of herself to put back together. She loved him just that much, and he had the power to either destroy her or make her deliriously happy. Emily knew that with Grady, there was nothing in between. It was all or nothing.

Trying to turn off her own thoughts, she went to the living room and turned on the Christmas tree that she and Grady had decorated together. It was Christmas Eve, and their dinner was warming, everything finished—including the huge turkey Grady had insisted on, telling her he'd eat the leftovers. Neither one of them talked about what would happen after Christmas. It was as though they were both afraid to burst the bubble of happiness that surrounded them right now.

The phone rang, startling Emily with its shrill ringtone. It was Grady's landline, and it hadn't rung once since she'd gotten here.

Walking to the kitchen, she wondered if she should answer. Grady had gone into Portland, telling her he had business to attend to, but that he'd be back by dinnertime.

It could be Grady. Maybe he's going to be late. Answer it.

The number was displayed as private, so she answered, fairly certain it was Grady. "Hello," she said cautiously.

"Where is Grady? And who are you?" a haughty female voice asked Emily.

"I'm sorry. He's not here. Can I take a message?" Uncomfortable, Emily shifted from foot to foot, wishing she hadn't picked up the phone.

"Who is this?" the female voice insisted in a nearly hostile voice.

"I'm Emily. I'm here to visit Grady for Christmas," she answered hesitantly, not wanting to piss off any of Grady's friends or business associates. "Can I tell him who called?" she inquired again.

Emily heard a sound of disgust before the woman answered, "I'm Hope Sinclair. Grady's wife. Get the hell out of my house." The line went dead with a loud, decisive *click*.

Her hands shaking, Emily dropped the phone back into the cradle. Her heart hammering so fast she could feel it pulsating through her body, she quickly turned off all the burners on the stove.

I have to go. I have to go.

The need to flee was clawing at her, adrenaline flooding her body.

I never asked him if he had someone. I just assumed he didn't.

There had never been any talk of Grady having a wife, but what did anyone really know about Grady Sinclair? He kept himself isolated, and maybe she traveled a lot. Or they could be separated. But he should have told her.

Pain sliced through her body, almost making her double over in agony. And with the pain came shame. She'd kissed another woman's husband, done intimate things with him.

"Oh, God," she whispered to herself in an anguished rasp.

No. No. No.

Emily couldn't breathe, couldn't think, wanting nothing more than to get out of the house. She needed air, and she needed to clear her whirling thoughts—none of them good, none of them rational.

"Noooo!" she wailed as she yanked the front door open, jammed her feet into her sneakers, and ran.

There was snow on the ground, but she ignored it, needing to distance herself from the pain that was cutting her to shreds. It was cold, but she'd be okay if she just kept running, just kept moving. Maybe she could outrun the agony of Grady's betrayal.

You don't know the truth. Don't jump to conclusions.

Her rational mind said it wasn't possible, but holy hell, her heart ached, and her eyes were streaming tears, the flow trickling down her face.

Why didn't he tell me?

She stopped, breathless and hopeless, at the shore. She made her way down a fishing dock that had been here as long as she could remember. It was weathered, but still sturdy. Standing at the end of the wooden structure, she looked out at the churning ocean. The sound of the crashing waves calmed her down a little, the turmoil matching the emotions that were slamming into her body all at once.

Pain.

Betrayal.

Fear.

Emptiness.

Despair.

Emily would have trusted Grady with her life, never imagining he'd hidden a secret that would destroy her.

The way he looked at me, the way he treated me . . . was everything a lie?

She really needed to leave before Grady got back. Part of her wanted to confront him, but she knew she needed time. She was hysterical, irrational. Her thoughts needed to be clear before she spoke with him or she'd lose it.

She had turned to leave, knowing she needed to go home and get herself together, when her foot skidded along the slippery, icy surface of the dock, making her lose her balance completely. One long slide, her slick sneakers propelling her sideways, and she tumbled into the churning waves with a startled, fearful scream.

Grady arrived just in time to hear Emily's scream of terror.

Following her footprints in the snow when he'd discovered she wasn't in the house, the trail had led him here to the dock. Her desperate cry had jerked his head to the end of the wooden structure, and before he could wonder what the hell she was doing on the slippery dock, she was falling.

"Fuck!" he rasped desperately, watching his whole life take a tumble into water that he knew couldn't be more than forty degrees.

He shed his jacket and sweatshirt on the run and dove into the water, the frigid temperature taking his breath away, but he ignored the stabbing pain of the impact. His only thought was to reach Emily.

She was bobbing near one of the dock posts, clinging to the wooden structure as the waves pounded at her body.

"What the hell are you doing?" Grady bellowed over the noise of the rushing water. "You have to get out of the water."

Jesus H. Christ, it was cold. He knew neither one of them would survive if they didn't get out of the water.

"My foot's stuck," she screamed. "Get out of the water, Grady."

He could see her struggling, her head going under to try to get free from whatever had her in its grasp.

"Get out of the water, my ass," he growled, diving under the waves and following her legs with his hand, keeping his other arm around the post to keep from being swept away from her by the waves.

The dock was old and weathered and her foot was lodged in a very large split in the wood, held in place by a bolt that was blocking her shoe from escaping. Grasping her foot tightly, he maneuvered it into a position where he could yank her foot free, coming to the surface gasping for air.

He didn't waste his breath trying to talk. He grasped Emily around the waist and propelled her toward the shore in front of him. The dock wasn't very long, and the waves helped, tossing them up on shore with very little effort.

Knowing he had to get them warm and dry, he scooped up Emily, wrapped her in his dry coat, and sprinted for the house, ignoring the pain of his circulation returning, and his clumsy motion. Jaw clenched with determination, he moved as fast as he could, clutching Emily tightly to his body.

I have to get her warm. She's not even shivering. She's hypothermic.

He didn't stop once he came through the door. He bolted up the stairs, and set Emily in the chair in his room, and frantically started to strip her down.

Her expression was blank, almost as if she were in shock. Grady tore her clothing as he removed it, desperate to get her out of her wet clothes. Once she was naked, he grabbed towels to dry her body and her hair hurriedly, deposited her in his bed, and started piling warm blankets on top of her. "You'll be warm in a few minutes, sweetheart. You'll be okay." He knew he was talking as much to himself as he was to her, trying to reassure himself that she was safe.

Her body started to shiver, and her teeth were chattering, which was a good sign. Her body temperature was rising.

"Get warm," she told him as she trembled beneath the blankets. "I'm okay."

She didn't look like she was okay at all, but her eyes looked up at him with a pleading expression that he couldn't ignore. He stripped hurriedly, his own body shivering, a reaction that he knew would raise his body temperature, but it was damn uncomfortable.

After using the towels to dry his own body, he slid beneath the pile of blankets. He doubted that he had much body heat, but he pulled Emily to him anyway, wondering if he could give her any warmth that he had left in his body through the sheer power of his will.

Grady clutched her against him, closing his eyes in relief as he felt them shivering together, their bodies warming.

What if I hadn't come home exactly when I did? What if I had made another stop? Would Emily have died out there, unable to get free?

A mammoth shudder went through his body, but it had nothing to do with his body temperature.

"What if I had lost you? What the hell were you doing out there? That dock isn't safe even in the summer." His voice was graveled and anxious.

Her teeth were still chattering slightly as she answered, "You'd still have your wife," she ground through her clenched teeth, struggling to move away from him.

Grady tightened his hold, not letting her escape. "What? Are you delusional? Talk to me." Maybe she was suffering worse than he thought, because she was uttering complete nonsense. But her body was settling down, and she was only shivering lightly now; his had stopped completely.

"Hope Sinclair," she said with a little more strength. "Your wife." She pummeled at his chest, trying to move away from him. "How could you, Grady? How could you kiss me and act like you cared about me when you have a wife tucked away somewhere? Was all of this just some kind of sick game for you? I was in love with you, you bastard!" Emily stopped fighting and burst into tears, her body starting to rock with heartbreaking sobs.

"Stop. Emily. Stop crying." *Christ!* He couldn't stand to see her this way. It was ripping his heart from his chest. "I don't have a wife. Hope is my sister. Did she call while I was gone?"

"Yes. She said she was your wife," she sniffed, the sobs halting. "Why would she say that if she wasn't?"

Grady snapped, the sight of Emily in tears unraveling him. He rolled Emily beneath him, trapping her so she couldn't go anywhere. "Because she knows Jared sends women who I don't want to hook up with me. She's helped me out before by claiming to be my wife to get rid of a few of them who didn't really want to take no for an answer." He loved his sister and he appreciated that she wanted to protect him from an unpleasant scene, but he wanted to wring her neck for not checking with him first.

"So you aren't . . . married?" Emily glanced at him for the first time, her expression vulnerable and shaken.

"She's my sister and I love her like a sibling, but I think being married to her is illegal just about everywhere in the world," he growled fiercely. "I'm fucking obsessed with you, or haven't you figured that out yet? I think about you every damn moment that I'm awake, and then I dream about you when I sleep. There is nobody else. And there never will be. I think I knew it the moment I saw you sitting in the snow on my doorstep. You're mine, angel. I need you more than I need anything else on this earth. Please don't leave me. Ever." His voice was vibrating with emotion, his eyes burning with a fire banked for far too long. Grady didn't care anymore if Emily owned his emotional well-being.

He'd already given it over to her, and she could do whatever she wanted with it. He was hers. And she belonged with him. "Nobody will ever love you as much as I do, or take care of you as well as I will. Stay with me, Emily. I need you."

Grady could feel his heart skip a beat as he waited for her answer.

Say yes. Say yes and I'll never want another Christmas gift as long as I live.

Her eyes were bright with tears as she nodded and murmured, "I love you, Grady Sinclair."

Grady took that answer as a yes because he wanted to, and it was the sweetest affirmation he'd ever heard. Right now, it was the only thing he needed to hear. He lowered his head and kissed her.

CHAPTER 8

Emily opened to him the moment his lips met hers, needing him to forgive her for doubting, for accusing him when he was innocent. She put her apology in her kiss, giving herself up totally to Grady. He'd kept her off balance from the moment they'd met, her usual rational thinking completely out the window. It wasn't possible to intelligently analyze the way she felt about Grady. It was as though their souls were entwined, and she was now whole since she'd met him, Grady filling a gaping crack in her soul that had always been empty.

Her once-chilled body burst into flames as Grady kissed her like a man possessed, his tongue entwining with hers, retreating, and then entering again with more force, demanding everything from her.

Yes. Yes. Yes.

His big body shuddered above her as she moaned into his embrace, her hands trying to touch him everywhere at once. Muscles rippled under her fingertips as she caressed down his back and grasped his rock-hard ass, trying desperately to urge him closer to her throbbing pussy. Pulling her mouth from his, she begged desperately, "Please, Grady. I need you."

"Not enough," Grady replied harshly. "But you will."

Pinning both hands over her head, he ran his tongue along the sensitive skin at the side of her neck and nipped her earlobe before adding,

"It took me thirty-one years to get a Christmas miracle, and you're worth it. So now I want to savor it," he told her in a graveled voice.

Helplessly, she ground her hips up, her pussy flooding as she felt his hard cock so close, but not close enough. "Savor later. Fuck now," she moaned, desperate to have Grady inside her.

"I want to do everything with you all at once. I've dreamed about this, sweetheart. I've dreamed about having you naked in my bed for so long, I'm about to lose my mind." He continued licking his way down her body, releasing her wrists and moving down to her breasts.

Emily gasped when he laved over one of her nipples, the sensitive peak responding to the feel of his wicked tongue. He pinched just hard enough to cause her body to jolt, the streak of electricity going straight to her pussy. And then he stroked her nipple with his tongue, sending a flood of warmth through her belly and into her core. "Fuck me, Grady. Please." If she didn't get him inside her, she was going to go completely mad. His body was sending off waves of heat, and they were about to consume her.

"Not yet. I need to taste you first," he replied huskily, his breath warm on her quivering belly. "And I promised to fuck you only if you begged."

Dear God, she was ready to grovel, ready to plead with him to have some mercy. There was only so much heat a woman could take, and she was already reaching her breaking point. "Grady . . . I can't . . . I don't," she stammered, unable to form a coherent thought as his mouth stroked over her wet folds, not quite getting to where she wanted him to be, but the feel of his wicked tongue made her hips thrust forward, so damn ready for him.

"You will," she heard him rumble, the vibrations pulsating against her pussy.

His fingers stroked down her outer thighs and came back up the sensitive skin on the inside, getting so very close. "Please." All she could feel was Grady, and the carnal things he was doing to her body. He was touching her, tasting her, breathing in her scent, and it was hot as hell. "Stop savoring. Need you now," she gasped, arching her back as she heard a satisfied groan as he dived in and she lost herself completely.

Grady might be a reclusive sort of guy outside of the bedroom, but there was no hesitation as he devoured her. He was completely uninhibited, tasting her with his entire mouth and tongue, feasting on her like he'd never be satiated.

"Oh . . . God . . ." Emily let go and a tortured sound escaped her lips as her ass came off the bed, offering herself up to him, needing more of Grady. She gripped the sheets of the bed, her knuckles white from the strength of her grasp.

He took her legs and pushed them up with her knees bent, opening her to him, completely exposing her to his erotic torment. His tongue lashed her throbbing clit, over and over, every pass driving her higher. No mercy. Grady was on a mission, his laser focus directed on making her come. Hard. And his complete domination of her body was making her come undone.

"You taste so sweet," he growled as he lifted his head. "You're almost ready to come for me."

Emily wanted to say she was beyond ready, but Grady was already completely consuming her again. "I can't do this . . . I can't . . ." Emily rasped, her heart galloping inside her chest, wondering if she was going to climax or die. Every muscle in her body was tense, and her orgasm was rushing toward her with frightening speed. It was as terrifying as it was intoxicating, her body never reacting this violently in the past.

It's all Grady. His touch makes me insane.

Her hands dove into his hair, grasping his head as he ate her relentlessly, his tongue now moving hot and heavy on her engorged clit. The tiny bud pulsated and her hips rocked with every stroke of his tongue.

Her eyes closed, and she saw flashes of light in the darkness, her whole body sensitized and electric. Her climax slammed into her like a hurricane, and she let out a moan of complete ecstasy as she found her release so hard that she was helpless to do anything else but lie there and come beneath Grady as he sipped at her climax like it was nectar.

"No more. Please. Fuck me." Emily was frantic, unable to wait another minute to feel Grady's cock inside her. She'd just experienced the most incredible orgasm of her entire life. Still, she needed . . . more. She needed Grady inside her.

Climbing up her body, Grady positioned himself between her thighs. His expression was possessive and animalistic, his eyes stormy and dark. "If I take you now, I'll never let you go," he warned her gutturally. "Not that I will anyway. You were mine since you landed on my doorstep, angel." He let his cock slide along her folds, drenching himself in her juices. "Just like this, you feel so good. So warm. So incredible." His hips moved, his shaft sliding through her folds again and again.

"I'm no angel. I'm just a woman who's going to go crazy if you don't fuck me right now." Emily ran her hands down his back and latched on to his fine ass, clawing at him, aching to have him claim her. "I'm begging, Grady. I need you."

"Condom," he growled against the side of her neck.

"I've been on birth control for years for my periods. Do you trust me?" she gasped.

"Hell, yes. And I'm damn glad you trust me, because I'm not sure if I could move right now. Nothing has ever felt this good," he said gruffly, and then swooped down to capture her mouth with his.

Emily could taste herself on his lips, and it only made her need him more. Her legs wrapped around his hips, urging him closer.

Grady entered her like his control had snapped, his cock embedding itself inside her to the hilt. He groaned, thrusting his tongue deeply into her mouth as his cock buried itself into her heat. He retreated and entered again, his groan even more tortured. Pulling his mouth from hers, he rasped, "You're so tight."

"It's been a while," she panted, wrapping her arms around his neck to hold on tight.

"Mine," he growled, his hips thrusting, his cock entering her again and again.

"Yes," she whispered harshly. "Oh, yes, Grady."

He took her body over, possessing her, claiming her with every stroke of his cock, touching places inside her that no one had ever touched before. He filled her completely, his pace increasing, his body demanding more and more. Emily gave him everything she had to give, moaning and throwing her head back as Grady slipped his hands beneath her ass and started to pummel himself into her with a force that took her breath away.

"Too hard. But I can't stop," he rumbled, sounding tortured.

"Don't stop. Take what you want. I'm right here with you." Emily loved his out-of-control dominance, and she didn't want him tame. "More," she pleaded, reveling in the feel of Grady's cock hammering in and out of her, claiming what belonged to him in the most elemental of ways.

"Love you, Emily," he said fiercely as he pumped into her over and over again.

She wanted to tell him she loved him too, but her climax hit her hard, rocking her body with intense spasms that robbed her of speech. She moaned incoherently, her channel clenching hard around Grady's cock.

His mouth covered hers, swallowing her sounds of ecstasy, and releasing his own groan as her climax milked him. His warm release exploded inside her as he kissed her senseless, as though he were trying to continue to claim her even after he already had her.

Releasing her mouth, he rolled, his cock disconnecting, her body splaying over his. They lay there together, both of them panting and out of breath. The moment she was able to speak, she blurted out, "I love you too. So very much."

He kissed her forehead, her lips, her cheeks, every spot on her face before he answered, "Stay with me, Emily. Every day will be like Christmas for me."

Emily swallowed back tears, hearing the vulnerability so very clear in his voice. "I want to give you Christmas every day. I want to make you happy, Grady."

"You already do," he said in a husky voice. He shifted her body gently to his side, covered her with the comforter and slid out of bed. Emily sighed as she watched his incredible body move across the room and take something out of the pocket of his soaked jeans.

"Damn. I lost my contacts in the water," she said, disgruntled, just now noticing that her vision was blurred.

Flipping on the light on the bedside table, Grady handed her a velvet box that was waterlogged and dirty. "I'll get you more. It doesn't matter. As long as you're safe. You took several years off my life, woman. You have to stop doing that. And I swear I'm going to clean out every store in the area to supply you with plenty of boots," he said gruffly. "Those sneakers are hazardous to my health."

Emily looked down at the box in her hand, her fingers starting to tremble.

"I wasn't really out on business. I needed to pick this up. I had a good friend who told me that I should marry you as soon as possible. I think it's the best advice that Simon ever gave me." He reached over and flipped open the box.

Emily's breath caught; the diamond inside the box was absolutely breathtaking. "Oh, my God."

"Marry me, angel?" He pulled the ring from its resting place and tossed the box on the floor.

Emily's tears began to flow like a river down her face. Grady didn't give her much time to answer as he lifted her hand and slipped the enormous diamond onto her finger. "Were you going to give me an option?" She hiccuped on a sob, her heart squeezing so tightly in her chest that she was short of breath.

"No," he answered, shooting her a wicked grin. "But a guy is supposed to ask."

Not able to wait a moment longer, Emily threw herself into his arms, hugging him so tightly she was probably choking him. But Grady didn't complain. He pulled her against him, holding her like he'd never let her go.

"It was going to be a yes anyway," she told him softly, laying her head against his shoulder.

"I know Hope can be convincing, but did you really think I had a wife?" Grady tilted her head up to look into her eyes.

"Honestly, I just reacted. I'm sorry. This is all pretty scary. I've never felt like this before, and I guess I just thought it was all too perfect to be real." She sighed, wondering now how she ever believed it as she looked into Grady's eyes, seeing the intensity of his love for her shining from their smoky depths. "I knew I could end up destroyed and hurt."

"No one will ever hurt you again," he answered hoarsely, his voice pulsating with emotion. Wrapping his arms around her, he pulled her into his lap. "If they do, I'll have to kill them."

Emily smiled against his shoulder, knowing Grady would always have protective, dominant instincts, but she wasn't complaining. His love would always surround her, and she would always feel the same protective feelings for him. "I'll shower you with so much love that you'll learn to love Christmas like I do someday," she told him confidently.

"I'm already liking it. It's Christmas Eve, and I'm pretty damn happy," he replied, his voice muffled against her hair.

"What would it take to make you love it?" She squirmed in his lap, feeling the hard, hot protrusion against her ass.

He moved at lightning speed, putting her on her back as he came over her, his eyes mischievous and wicked. Moving between her thighs, he pinned her hands over her head. "You . . . in my bed . . . all night long and all day tomorrow. I think I'd be deliriously happy by the end of tomorrow and love Christmas. I might just stroll through Amesport handing out candy canes and wishing everyone as merry of a Christmas as I just had."

Emily laughed merrily. "I think I'd like to see that."

"You know how to accomplish it," he challenged.

"I promised to show you a merrier Christmas," she said thoughtfully.

"Yeah. Yeah, you did." Grady swooped down and kissed her before adding, "But I thought you weren't going to do what we just did."

"No woman could resist a Christmas present like you," Emily told him with a contented sigh.

Grady broke into a sexy smile that melted her heart, and then he kissed her, a Christmas kiss that promised her forever.

They never made it out of bed until the next evening, and they were both so happily exhausted that it was all they could do to eat, and then take themselves straight back to bed, the candy canes completely forgotten.

But it was the merriest Christmas Grady and Emily had ever had.

EPILOGUE

One week later, Grady found himself back at the Youth Center, but he wasn't exactly going reluctantly anymore. Grady Sinclair was throwing a party, and he was actually the host. He'd had very little time to arrange it, but he'd pulled off a pretty decent New Year's Eve bash.

The party was in full swing, the band he'd hired filling the hall with music that had most of the folks of Amesport out on the makeshift dance floor.

He smiled as he watched Emily hugging her parents and laughing. God, she made him happy, and he felt every possessive instinct in his body stand at attention when he saw the flash of his ring on her finger, almost unable to believe she was really his.

Her mom and dad had been surprised when Grady's private jet had picked them up at the airport, but they had taken everything in stride. They'd come to meet him and attend the party to make their daughter happy. Really, Grady thought that was pretty extraordinary. Maybe it was normal behavior for loving parents, but normal was something he'd never experienced with his own mother and father.

Honestly, his childhood *had* been fucked up, but Emily made up for all that and more. If he had to do it again just to find his way to her, he'd do it in a heartbeat. He'd moved to Amesport to finally try to find some peace. Since he'd already owned property on the peninsula, he'd thought the small town would be the perfect place to avoid people. But he realized that real happiness couldn't be found in a location. His real joy was Emily, and he was quickly realizing that all people were not like his father, that he really didn't need to isolate himself. He might never be a social animal, but he wasn't afraid of people anymore. Emily loved him. If she could accept him, maybe others could as well.

Grady's eyes strayed to the other side of the room, watching his siblings all gathered together, looking like they were actually enjoying the party, maybe because it had brought them all together again. Hope had come from Aspen, minus her loser boyfriend, and his brothers Evan, Dante, and Jared had all arrived together a short time ago. Even Jason had showed up, claiming he had nothing better to do for New Year's Eve.

Grady's eyes narrowed on Dante, noticing how exhausted his brother looked. Dante, a year younger than Grady, had taken his own path after he'd left the Sinclair home when he was eighteen. He'd gone to college for a criminal justice degree, joining the police force in Los Angeles, quickly and aggressively moving up the ranks to become a homicide detective. Was he happy? Grady noticed the dark circles under Dante's eyes, and the weary expression on his face. Maybe Dante had just been working crazy hours lately, but Grady had a feeling that Dante probably looked exactly the same most of the time. How could he not? Dante worked homicide in the worst district in Los Angeles for murders, many of them gang related. That kind of job had to eventually take its toll on a cop.

His wayward thoughts were interrupted as Emily came toward him, her hips swaying in a red cocktail dress that he really thought should be illegal. It clung to her curves and exposed more skin than he thought she should be showing, but she looked so incredibly hot that he was hard the instant she smiled at him.

"I still can't believe you arranged all this. God, you look gorgeous in a tuxedo." She wrapped her arms around his neck and planted a soft kiss on his lips. "You're amazing, Mr. Sinclair."

Grady raised a brow at her, knowing a challenge when he was confronted with it. "I thought I told you that I'd make you pay for calling me that. There's a lot of Sinclairs. I want to be special."

"You never told me exactly how that punishment would work." She'd moved closer, talking to him in her *fuck-me* voice, right next to his ear. "I might like it."

Okay . . . the party had been a great idea, and it had made his woman happy, but he was ready to take her home now. "I'll show you when we get home." Thank God all of his siblings had their own places.

"Hope apologized. Poor thing. She was mortified when she heard what happened. You shouldn't have told her," Emily scolded lightly. "I like her. I like all of your family."

"It seems strange, all of us together again." Grady wrapped his arms around Emily's waist. "I missed them."

"Maybe they can stay for a while," Emily said hopefully.

"Don't get your hopes up," Grady warned her with a frown. "It's a miracle that we're just all in the same place right now."

"One minute to midnight," a happy male voice pronounced loudly, making himself heard over the music.

Grady snagged two glasses of champagne from a nearby table and brought one to Emily. His siblings, Jason, and Emily's parents all gathered around them, and Grady's heart felt as full as it could possibly get. He was here with the woman he loved, all of their family around them. It just didn't get any better than this.

"I can't wait until later," Emily whispered into his ear in sultry voice.

Okay . . . maybe it *could* get better later, but he was still pretty damned contented.

"Are you tipsy?" he asked Emily with a smile. She'd told him earlier that she got a little wild when she drank, so he'd made damn sure her glass was full all evening.

"Maybe just a tiny bit," she admitted, holding up her index and thumb with a fair amount of space in between.

"Five."

"Four."

"Three."

"Two."

"One."

The entire hall exploded with cheers, the New Year being properly greeted by the people of Amesport.

After Emily had hugged everyone in the family and bussed them all on the cheek, she grabbed Grady's hand and tugged him onto the dance floor. "Dance with me," she insisted, throwing her slightly intoxicated self into his arms without inhibition.

Grady swooped her up into his arms, letting her feet float slowly back down to the floor. "Happy New Year, angel."

"Happy New Year, love," she answered, her eyes glowing with happiness. "Tell me your New Year's wishes and I'll make them all come true," she told him with conviction.

Grady smiled down at her. "I wish that you would love me forever."

She smacked him playfully on the arm before letting him swing her into a dance to "Auld Lang Syne." "You already have *that*. Think of something else."

"Impossible, angel. You already made anything I could wish for come true."

Her eyes started to shine with unshed tears. "I love you, Grady."

He pulled her closer and whispered into her ear, "I love you too. Thank you for giving me back the holidays. What's your New Year's wish?" He wanted desperately to give Emily anything she wished for and more.

"I wish that you would kiss me," she answered simply.

"I'm a billionaire, and that's the only thing you wish for?" He smirked, but his heart was secretly singing.

"It's what I want. You told me you'd try to give me anything I wanted," she told him in a mischievous voice, tossing his own words back at him.

"Anything you want, sweetheart," he answered, his voice amused.

Two seconds later, Grady had Emily bent over his arm, and he made damn sure that he gave her the sweetest, most passionate New Year's kiss she'd ever had.

NO ORDINARY BILLIONAIRE

BY J. S. SCOTT

HERE'S A SNEAK PEEK AT THE FIRST FULL-LENGTH BOOK IN THE SINCLAIRS SERIES

CHAPTER 1

It was completely annoying that it had been sunny and bright on the day of Patrick's funeral. Not one single cloud in the sky as a sea of men in uniform, their badges all covered with a black, horizontal stripe to mark the loss of one of their own, milled around a cemetery. Their expressions were solemn, and many of them were visibly sweating from wearing a heavy uniform in the Southern California heat.

Detective Dante Sinclair's eyes were riveted to the screen as he watched the video on his laptop computer, a huge lump in his throat as he listened to the customary last radio call go out for Detective Patrick Brogan, unanswered. Patrick was officially proclaimed to be 10/7, out of service, and the dispatcher declared how much he would be missed.

Dante gulped for air as he slammed the laptop closed, wishing like hell that it had been a shitty, rainy day during the funeral. Somehow it didn't seem fair that the services had been held on just the kind of day Patrick had loved, and he hadn't been there to enjoy it. It was just the sort of weather that would have had Patrick itching to be out fishing. Instead, he'd been dead, entombed in a casket covered by a United States flag, unable to enjoy one single thing he loved ever again.

Casting the laptop off the bed, not caring whether it shattered into pieces, he sat up, unconcerned with the pain it caused him to do so. *Christ!* He hadn't even been able to attend his own partner's funeral because he'd still been in the hospital. But he'd been compelled to watch it. Patrick had been his partner and a member of Dante's homicide team for years. He'd also been the closest friend Dante had ever had.

It should have been me who died. Patrick had a wife, a teenage son who was left behind without a father.

Hell, Karen and Ben, Patrick's wife and son, had practically adopted him, having him over for dinner almost every night when he and Patrick could actually manage to catch dinner—which wasn't often. Their jobs kept them out at all hours, especially in the evenings. Murder rarely happened during the daytime hours in his district.

Karen and Ben will never have to worry about money. It won't make up for the loss of Patrick, but it will help.

Dante had resolved any financial problems for Karen and Ben by donating several million dollars to a fund for the Brogan family anonymously, but it wouldn't bring back the man they loved, the husband, the father. It seemed like a pitifully small thing to do considering he had plenty of money and would never miss it.

Although he and Patrick had gotten promoted to detective at the same time, Dante's partner had been well over a decade older, and a hell of a lot wiser than Dante had been back then. Patrick had taught a hotheaded new detective patience when Dante had none, and he'd helped Dante become a better man in more ways than he could count.

Christ! It should have been me! Why I wasn't I standing where Patrick had been standing when the shooter opened up and fired?

He and Patrick had been so close—so damn close—to nailing a murderer who had raped and killed three women in their rough, gang-populated division. They had been tailing the suspect on the street, waiting for backup to arrive to arrest the subject. The murderer had gotten sloppy on his last victim, leaving behind enough DNA evidence to finally arrest the bastard.

Swinging his legs painfully over the side of the bed, Dante relived the last few moments of Patrick's life, flashing back to the instant where he'd lost his best friend.

He and Patrick staying close enough to keep the suspect in their sight.

The piercing sirens nearby screeching through the air.

The suspect suddenly panicking and pulling out a semiautomatic pistol and starting to shoot.

Why the suspect had suddenly cracked at that moment was still a mystery. The sirens had probably spooked a murderer who already knew the law was on his tail and closing in. Ironically, the sirens had had nothing to do with them taking down a murderer. They'd been wailing for a completely separate incident. Like the police were really going to announce they were coming for the asshole? Still, it had been enough to send the suspect over the edge, shooting at anyone or anything behind him without warning.

Patrick had been the first to fall, with one bullet through the head. Dante had pulled out his Glock as he took several bullets from the shooter at close range, shielding Patrick with his larger body until he'd managed to get a kill shot in on the asshole shooter. At the time, Dante hadn't realized it was already too late for Patrick. The bullet through the head had killed his partner instantly. Luckily, the few civilians who had been hanging around on the street during the early morning hours had scattered, leaving Dante the only one injured—Patrick and the suspect both dead.

He'd been wearing his vest, but the close-range shots had caused him some blunt force trauma. However, it *had* saved his life, leaving him with only some cracked ribs instead of bullets through his chest. The shot to his face hadn't entered his skull, leaving him with only a nasty wound to his right cheek that extended up to his temple. The bullet to his right leg had passed through the flesh of his thigh, putting him in surgery after the incident, but it hadn't shattered the bone. The one to his left arm had just been a graze.

Lucky bastard!

Dante could almost hear his partner's voice saying those exact words to him jokingly, but he was feeling far from fortunate at the moment. He'd been injured badly enough to spend a week in the hospital, unable to attend Patrick's funeral, unable to say a final good-bye to his best friend. Karen and Ben had visited him after his surgery, Patrick's wife tearfully telling him how glad Patrick would have been that Dante had survived, and actually thanking him for trying to protect her husband. Neither one of them blamed Dante for what had happened to their beloved husband and father, yet Dante couldn't get past the fact that he wished it would have been him instead of his partner, that he had somehow let Patrick down by not being the one to die.

Survivor's guilt.

That's what the department psychologist was calling it, telling Dante it was common considering the circumstances. That comment had made Dante want to send the little head-shrinking bastard across the room with his fist. What the hell was normal about wishing himself dead?

"You okay?" His brother Grady's low, concerned voice came from the doorway of the small bedroom. "Need anything? We're only about an hour out from landing. I thought I heard something crash in here."

It was ironic that Dante and his siblings had always wanted to protect Grady—too often unsuccessfully—from being the primary target of their alcoholic, abusive father. And now *Grady* was the brother who was trying to take care of *him*. Every single one of his siblings had been at the hospital in Los Angeles, having flown in as soon as they had heard that he was injured. But he was going with Grady to his vacation home in Maine, a house he owned but had only seen briefly a few times since it had been constructed. Every one of the Sinclair siblings had a home on the Amesport Peninsula, but only Grady had actually made his house a permanent home. Dante hoped he could escape there, stop reliving the last moments of Patrick's life in his nightmares. Right now, the only thing he could see every time he closed his eyes was Patrick dying.

They were currently in flight on Grady's private jet, making their way from Los Angeles to Amesport, Maine. They'd be landing in a smaller airport outside of the city limits.

"I could use a beer," Dante told Grady in a tortured voice, not looking at his brother as he buried his face in his hands. "Ouch! Shit!" Dante moved his hands away, the pain of the still-tender wound on his face irritated by his actions.

"Alcohol and painkillers don't mix," Grady mentioned calmly as he picked up the laptop from the floor. Miraculously, the computer was still working, and Grady frowned as he opened the top and saw what his brother had been viewing. "You were watching the funeral? We were all there, Dante. I know you feel like shit because you couldn't be there. Every one of us went for you because you couldn't."

They all had, and the fact that his brothers and sister had attended the funeral for him to pay their last respects to a man they never even knew touched him deeper than they would ever know. They'd stood in his place, united in their support of him at Patrick's funeral. It had meant a hell of a lot, but . . .

"I had to see it myself." Dante looked up his older brother, his expression stony. "And I'm not taking the painkillers." Maybe it was stupid, but feeling the pain of his injuries seemed to somehow make him feel less guilty that he was still alive. If he was fucking hurting, he was paying the price of still being alive while Patrick was buried six feet under.

The psychologist thought he was having self-destructive thoughts.

Dante didn't give a shit.

"Hold on," Grady answered gravely, leaving briefly and coming back with a bottle of beer. He screwed off the top and handed it to Dante. "It's not exactly the healthiest thing for you to have right now, but I doubt it will do much harm."

Tossing his head back, Dante took a gulp of the cold liquid, letting it slide down his throat, suddenly questioning the intelligence of doing so. The taste brought back a flood of memories, all of them about the many times over the years that he and Patrick had hung out together having a beer. He finished it quickly as Grady watched him pensively, handing the empty bottle back to his brother after he drained it. "Thanks."

Grady took the bottle from Dante's hand with an uneasy scowl. "Are you okay?" he asked again in a husky voice. "I know your wounds hurt like hell, but they'll heal. That's not what I'm asking. I need to know if *you're* okay."

Dante finally looked up at his older brother, the concern on Grady's face nearly breaking him. Although the Sinclair siblings had all scattered to different areas of the country after they'd left their hellish childhood and adolescence behind, the affection they all had for one another had never died. They might only get together on rare occasions, but they all still cared. He had seen it in every one of his siblings' eyes at the hospital.

The anxiety and distress that was lodged deeply in Grady's gray eyes finally made Dante admit for the first time, "No. I don't think I am."

Patrick was dead. Dante wished he had died in his place. His body was wracked with pain, and everything inside him was cold and dark.

Right at that moment, as his anguished eyes locked with his older brother's, Dante wasn't sure he would ever be okay again.

ABOUT THE AUTHOR

Photo © 2013 by Carrie Herzog

J. S. (Jan) Scott is a *New York Times* and *USA TODAY* bestselling author of steamy romance. She's an avid reader of all types of books and literature. Writing what she loves to read, Jan writes both contemporary and paranormal romance. They almost always feature an alpha male and every book has a happily ever after because she just can't seem to write them any other way! Jan lives in the Colorado Rocky Mountains with her husband.